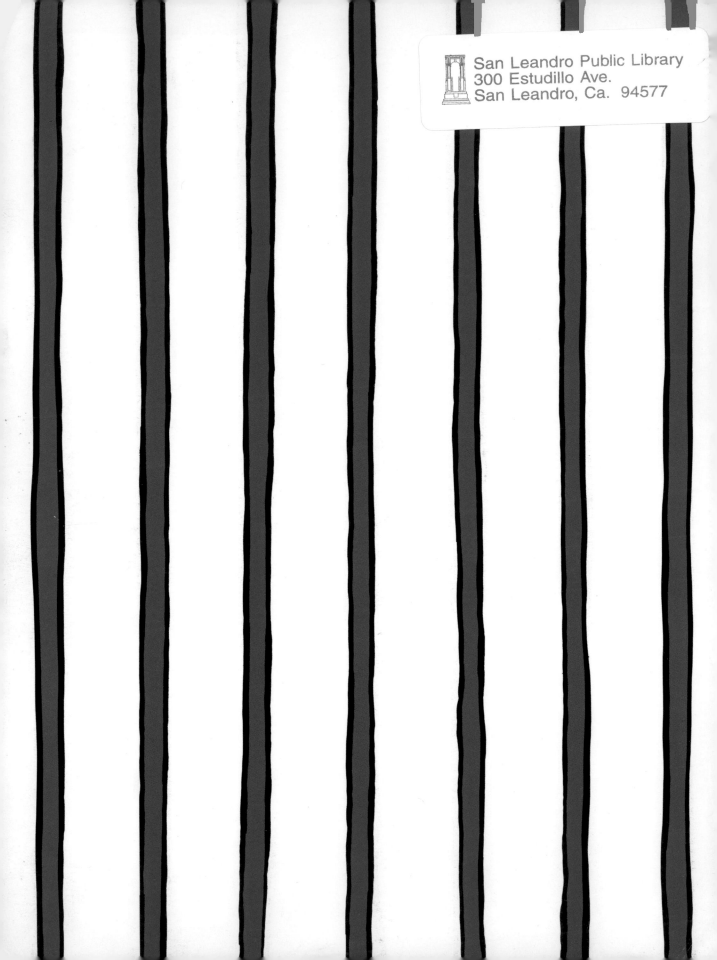

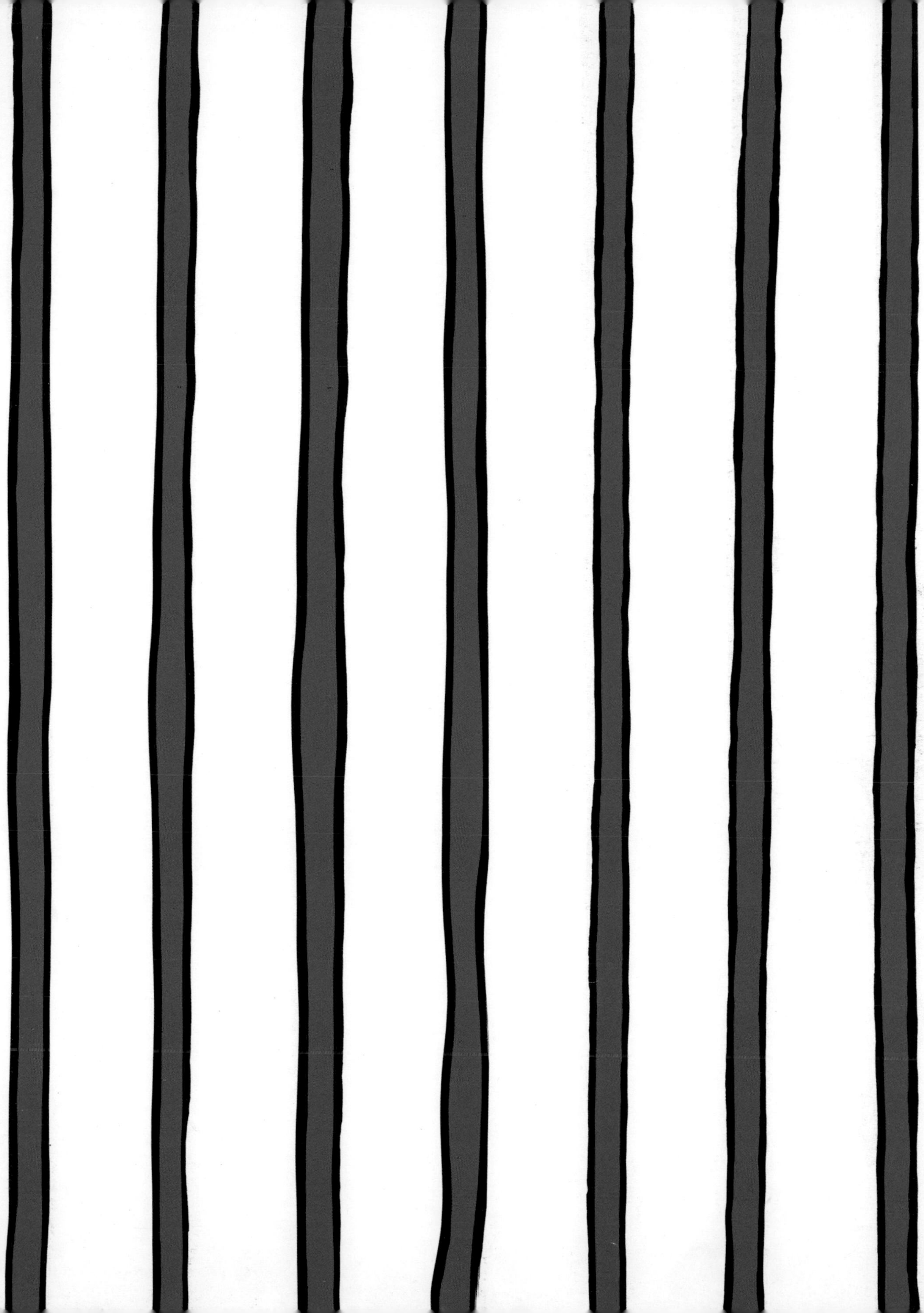

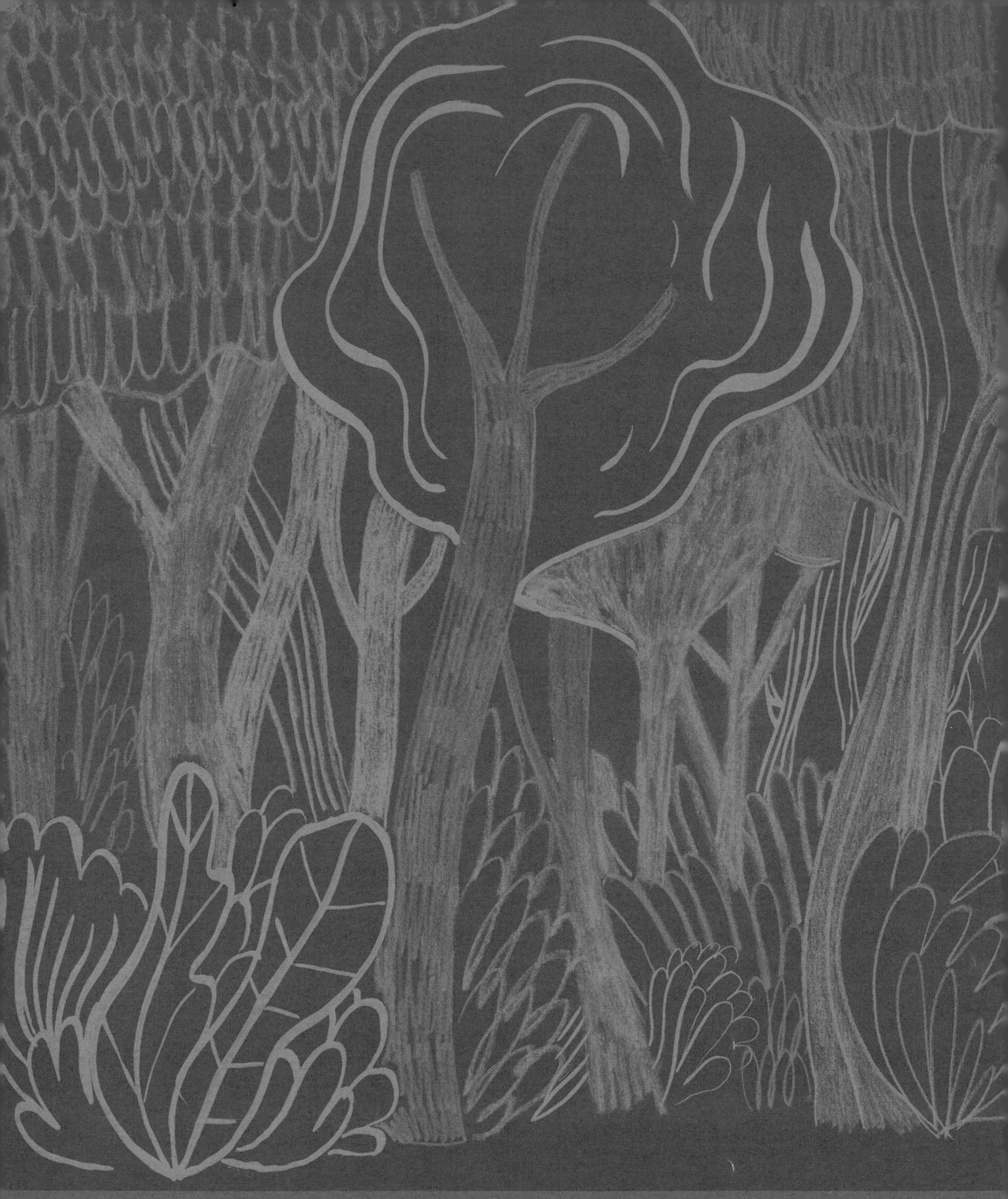

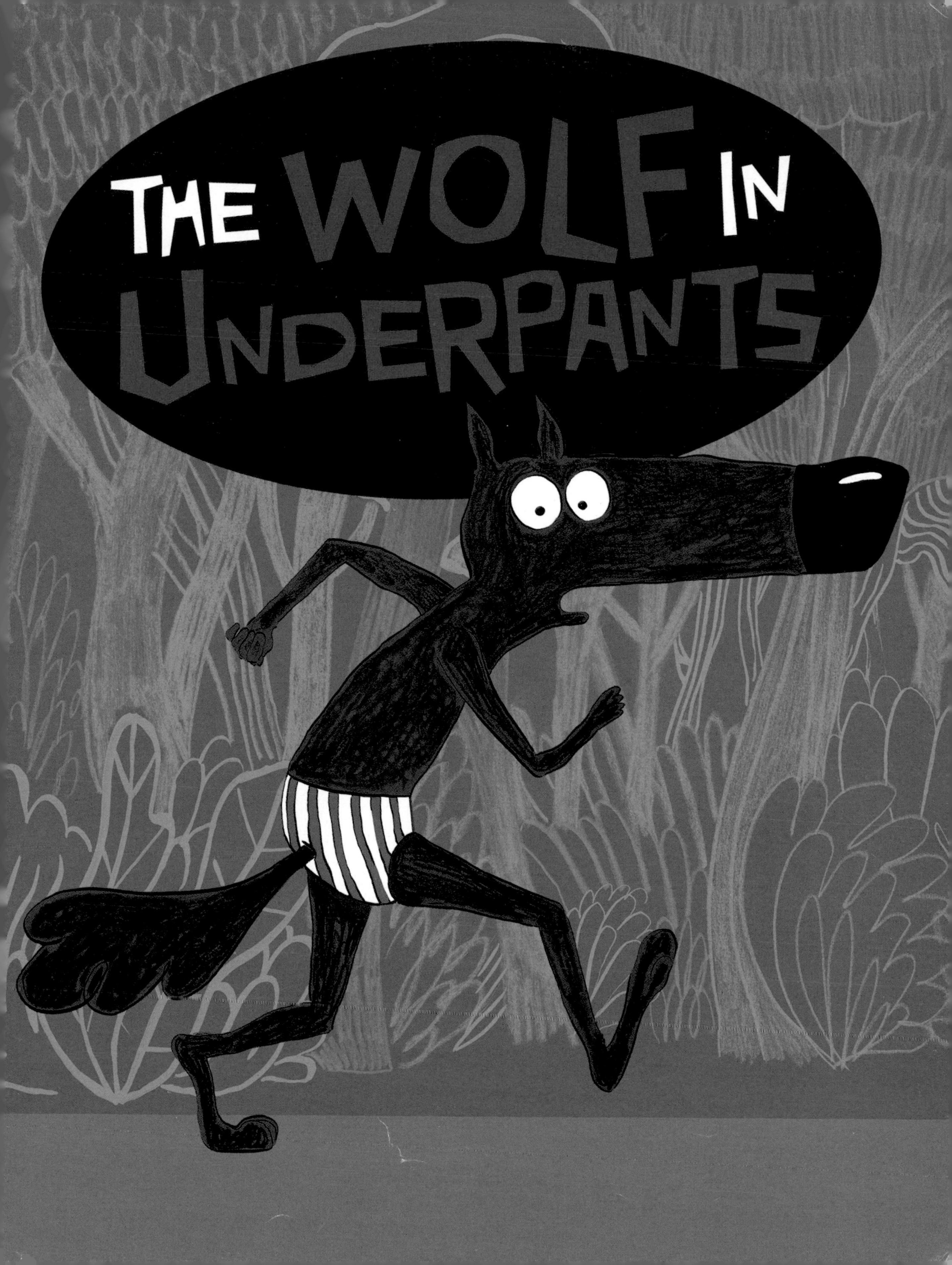
THE WOLF IN
UNDERPANTS

Story by Wilfrid Lupano
Art by Mayana Itoïz
With the friendly artistic participation of Paul Cauuet
Translation by Nathan Sacks

First American edition published in 2019 by Graphic Universe™
Published by arrangement with Mediatoon Licensing - France
Le Loup en Slip
© Dargaud Benelux (Dargaud-Lombard S.A.) 2016—Lupano, Itoïz, and Cauuet. All rights
reserved. Original artistic director: Philippe Ravon.
www.dargaud.com

Graphic Universe™
A division of Lerner Publishing Group, Inc.
241 First Avenue North
Minneapolis, MN 55401 USA

For reading levels and more information, look up this title at www.lernerbooks.com.

Main body text set in Stick-A-Round 13/15. Typeface provided by Pintassilgoprints.

Library of Congress Cataloging-in-Publication Data

Names: Lupano, Wilfrid, 1971- author. | Itoïz, Mayana, 1978- illustrator. | Cauuet, Paul,
    1980- illustrator. | Sacks, Nathan, translator.
Title: The wolf in underpants / Wilfrid Lupano, Mayana Itoïz, Paul Cauuet.
Other titles: Le Loup en slip
Description: First American edition. | Minneapolis : Graphic Universe, 2019. | "Translation by
    Nathan Sacks"—Title page verso. | Summary: After living in fear of the wolf with crazy
    eyes and fangs like ice picks, a forest community is stunned when he shows up looking
    calm and wearing striped underpants, leaving them wondering why they were so afraid
    of him.
Identifiers: LCCN 2018014450 (print) | LCCN 2018021439 (ebook) | ISBN 9781541542730
    (eb pdf) | ISBN 9781541528185 (lb : alk. paper) | ISBN 9781541545304 (pb : alk. paper)
Subjects: LCSH: Graphic novels. | CYAC: Graphic novels. | Wolves—Fiction. | Forest animals—
    Fiction. | Fear—Fiction.
Classification: LCC PZ7.7.L86 (ebook) | LCC PZ7.7.L86 Wo 2019 (print) | DDC 741.5/973—dc23

LC record available at https://lccn.loc.gov/2018014450

Manufactured in the United States of America
1-44701-35532-6/8/2018

THE WOLF IN UNDERPANTS

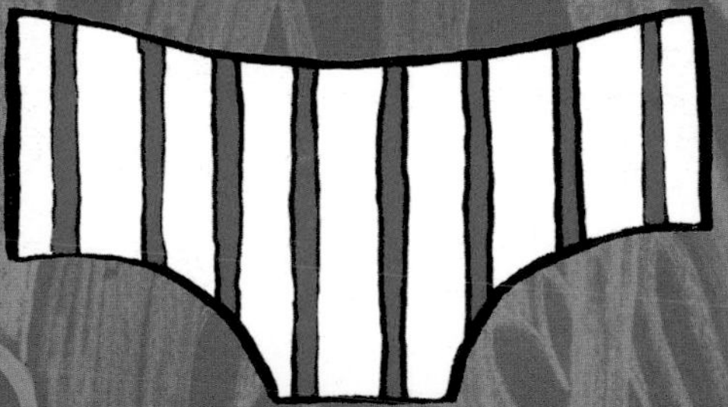

Wilfrid Lupano

Mayana Itoïz
and
Paul Cauuet

Graphic Universe™ • Minneapolis

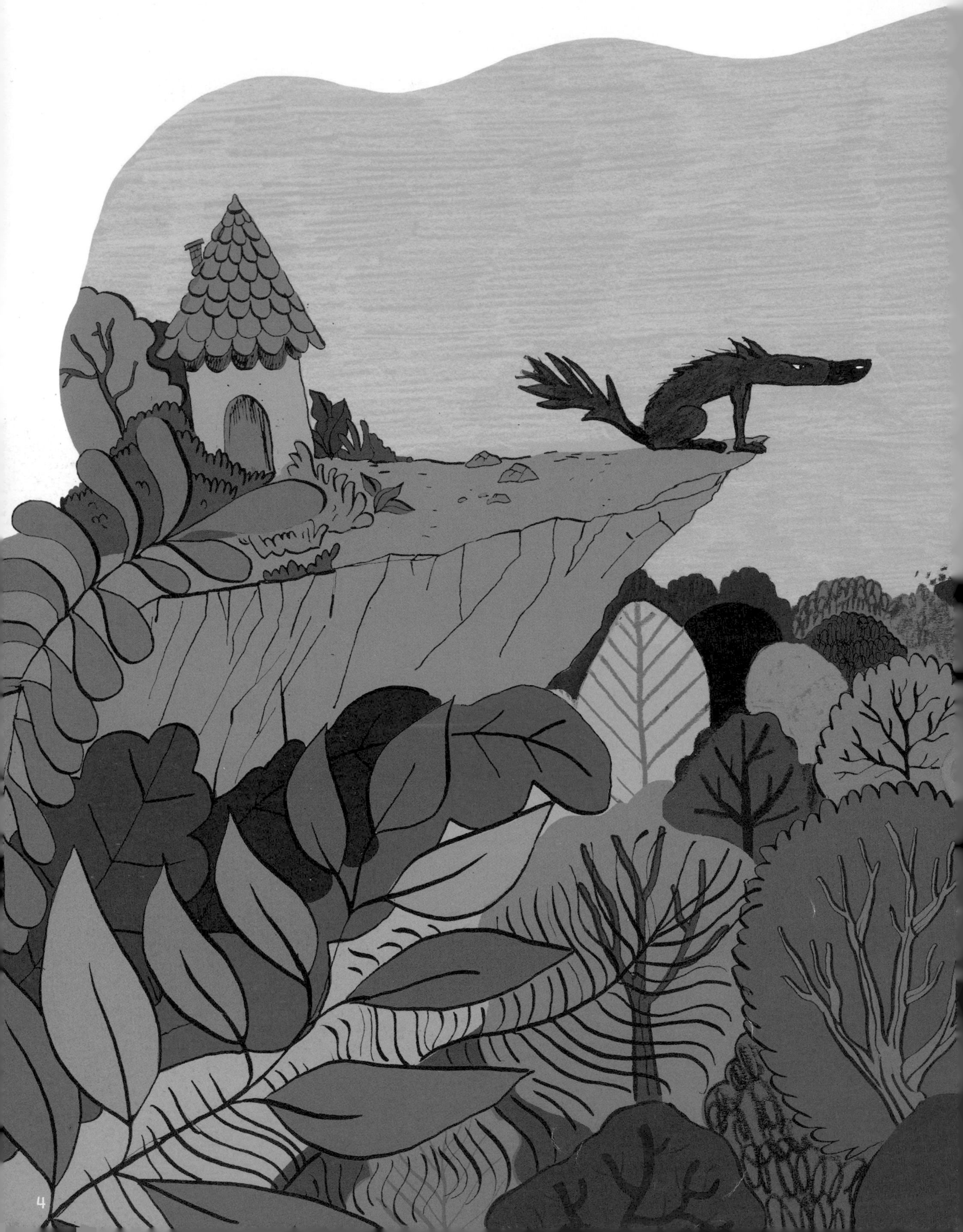

HIGH ABOVE THE FOREST LIVES THE WOLF. AN ICY CRY. CRAZY EYES.

IN THESE WOODS, WE KNOW TO MOVE OUR BUTTS WHEN THE WOLF COMES DOWN TO EAT.

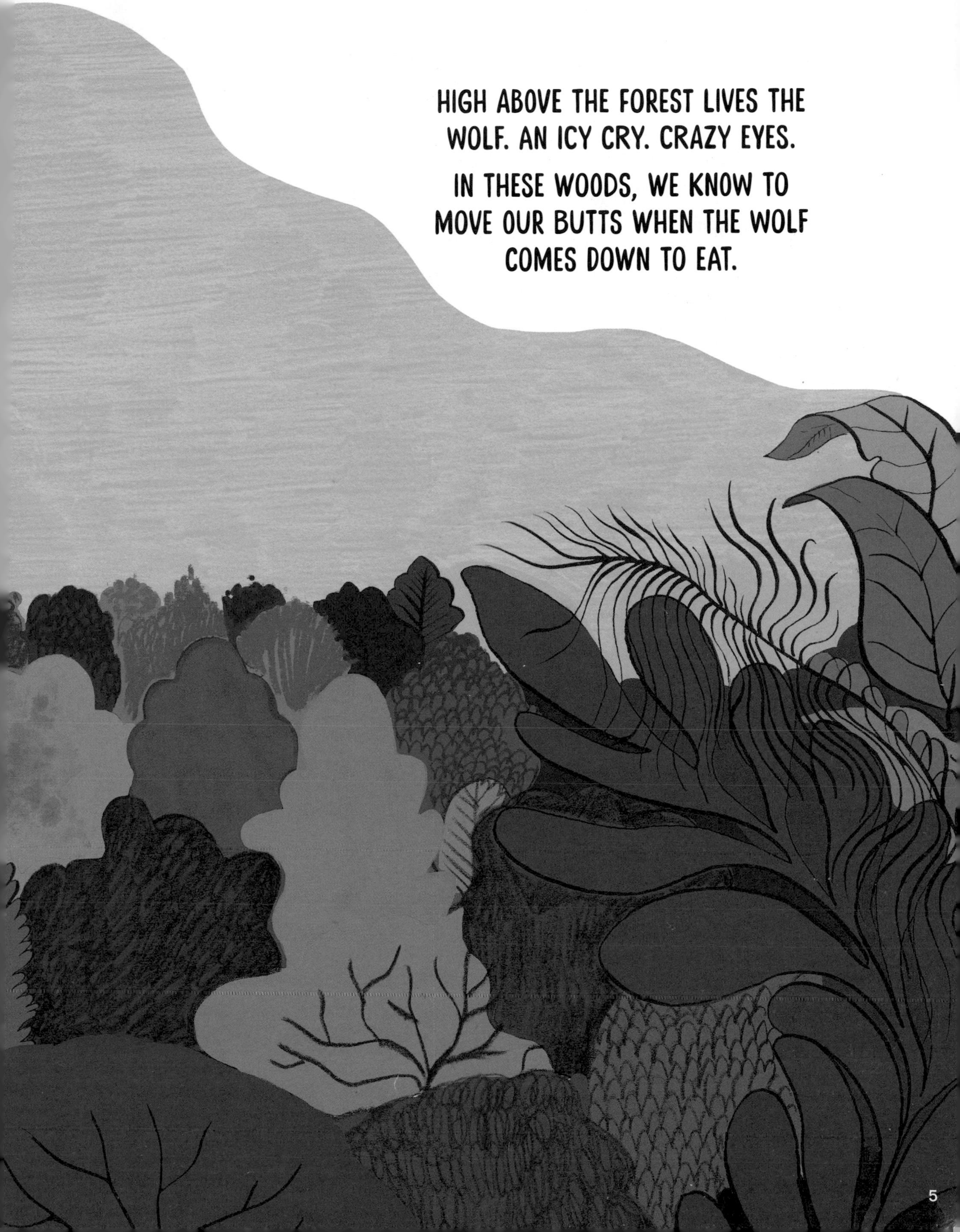

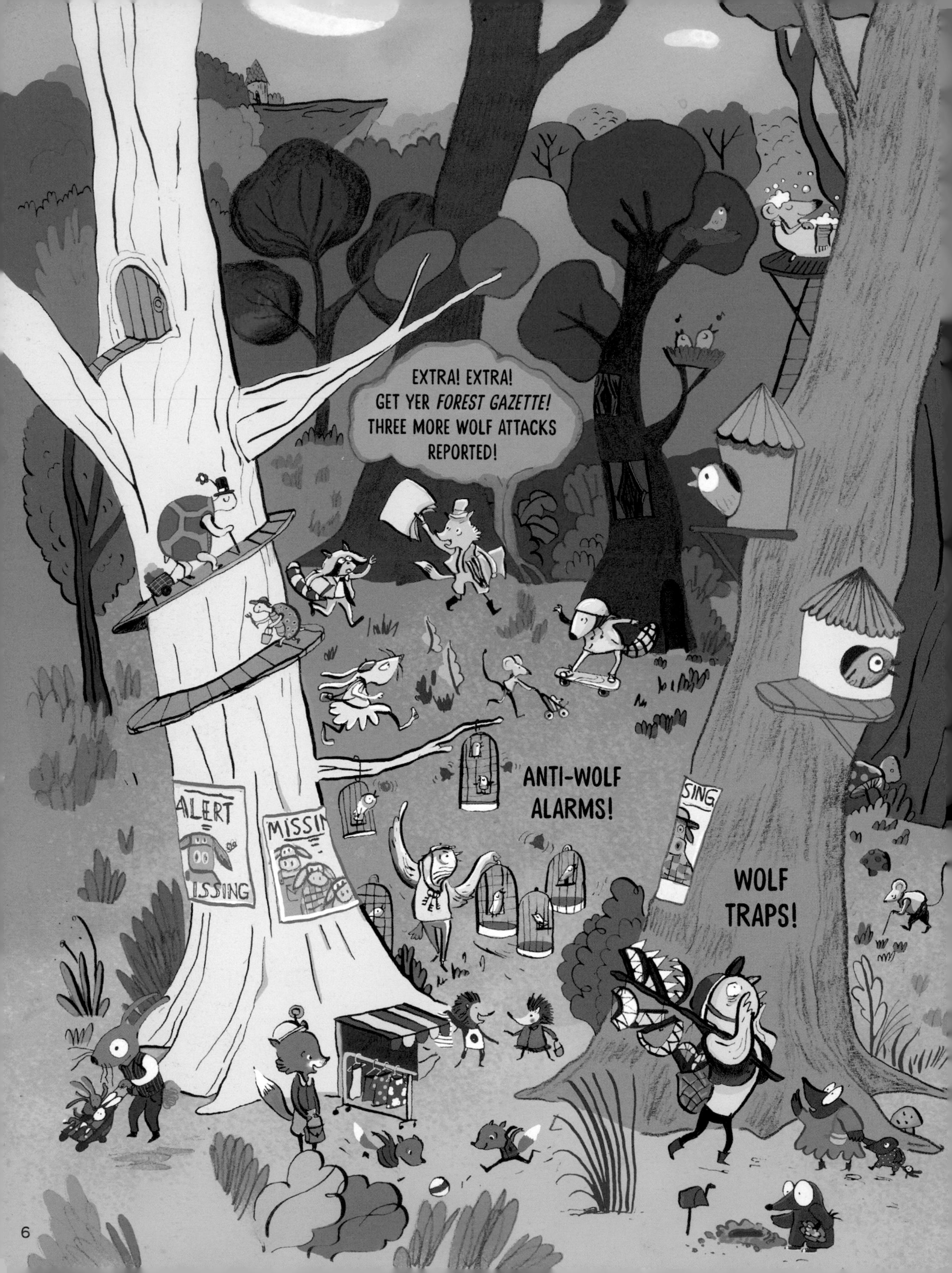

EXTRA! EXTRA!
GET YER *FOREST GAZETTE*!
THREE MORE WOLF ATTACKS
REPORTED!
ALERT
ISSING
MISSIN
SING
ANTI-WOLF
ALARMS!
WOLF
TRAPS!

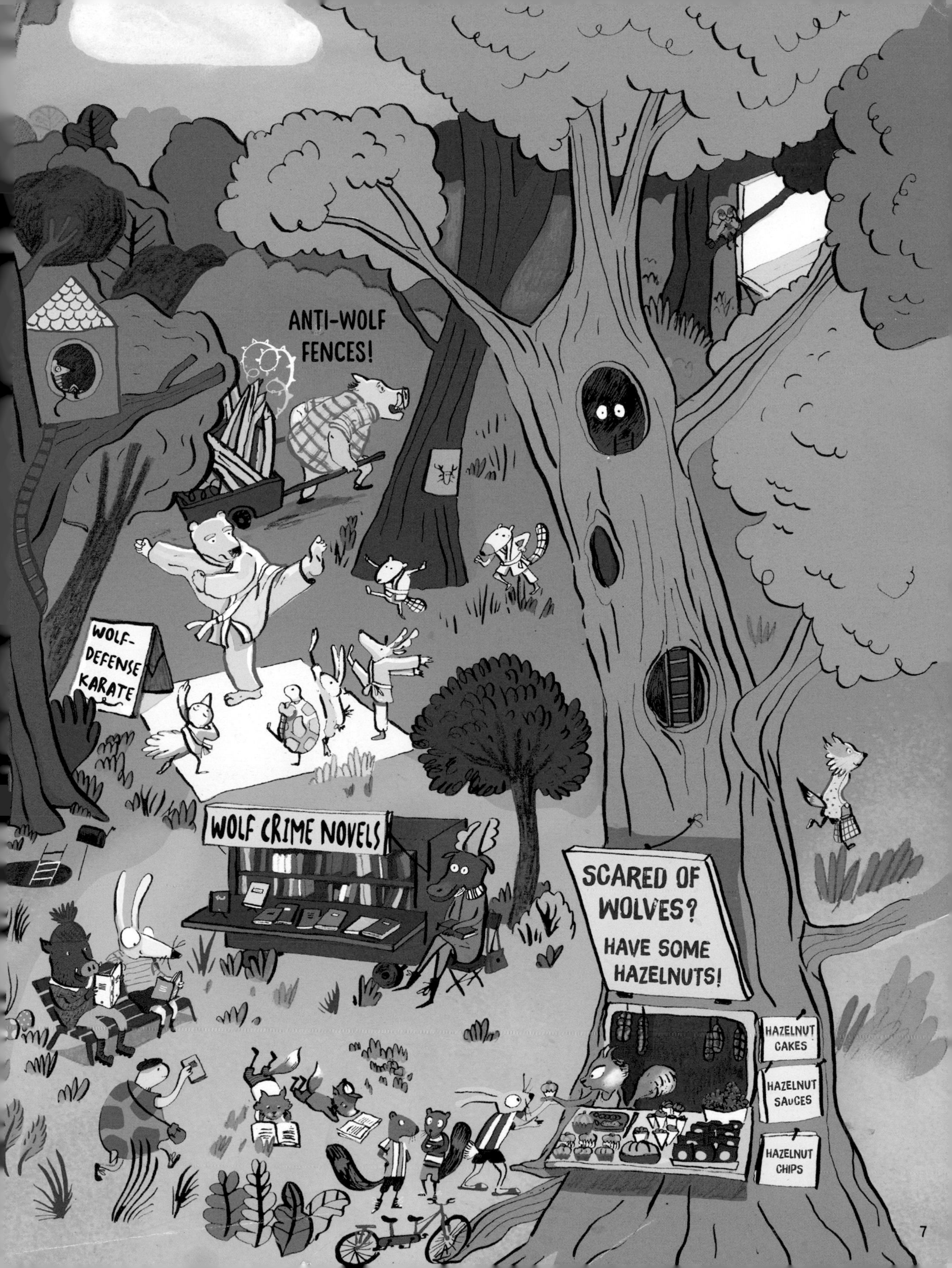
ANTI-WOLF FENCES!
WOLF-DEFENSE KARATE
WOLF CRIME NOVELS
SCARED OF WOLVES?
HAVE SOME HAZELNUTS!
HAZELNUT CAKES
HAZELNUT SAUCES
HAZELNUT CHIPS

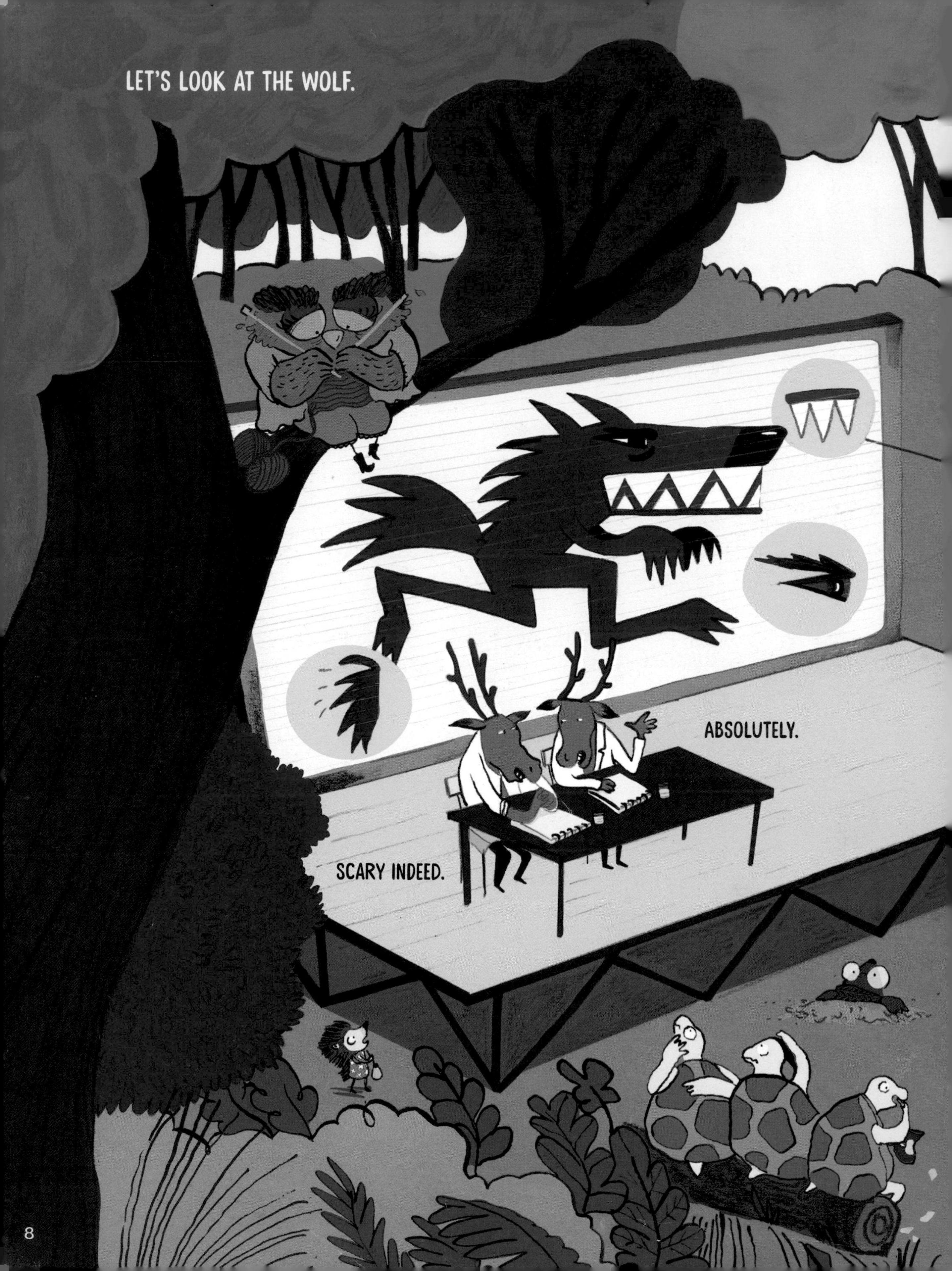
LET'S LOOK AT THE WOLF.
ABSOLUTELY.
SCARY INDEED.

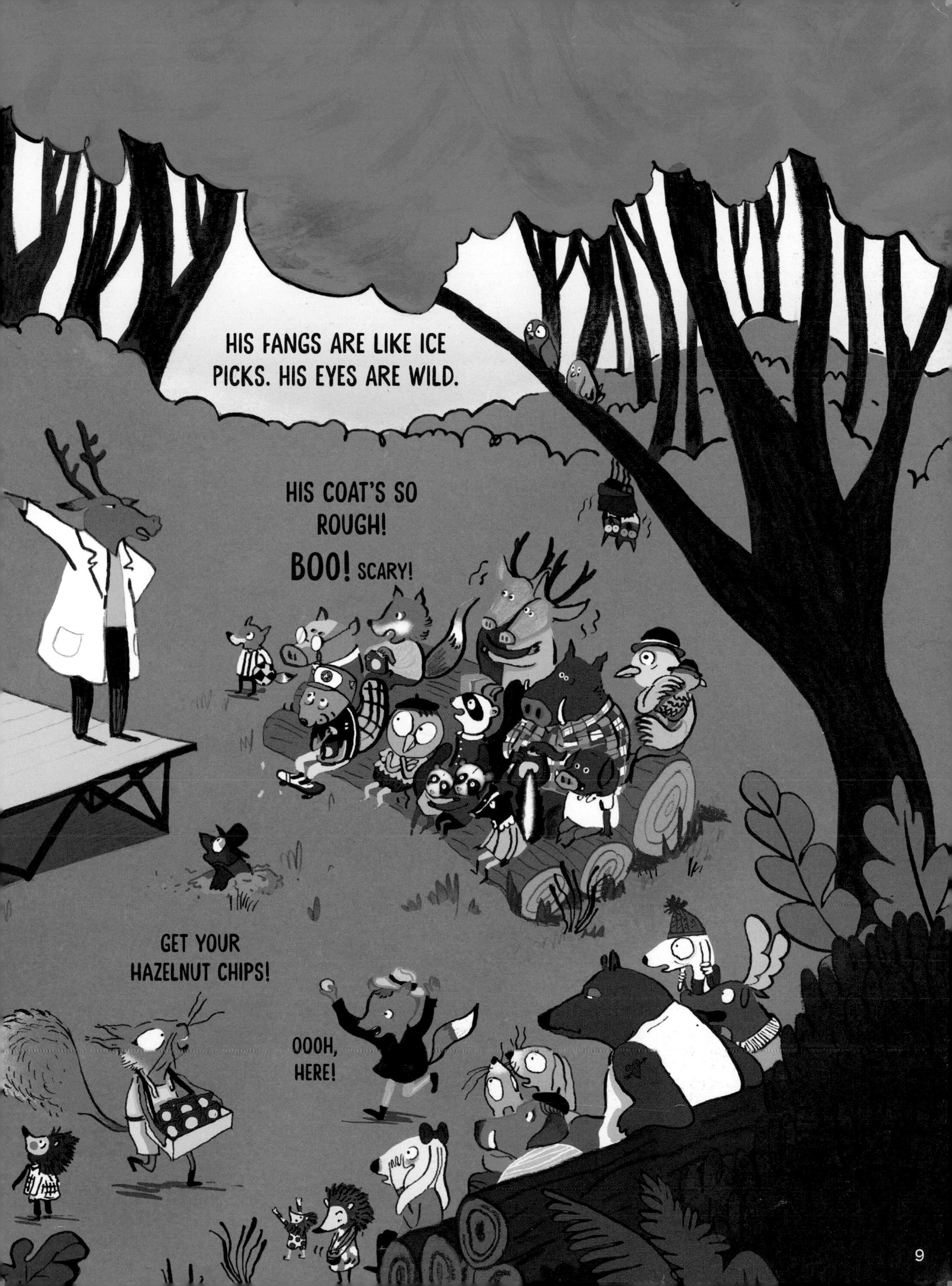
HIS FANGS ARE LIKE ICE PICKS. HIS EYES ARE WILD.
HIS COAT'S SO ROUGH!
BOO! SCARY!
GET YOUR HAZELNUT CHIPS!
OOOH, HERE!

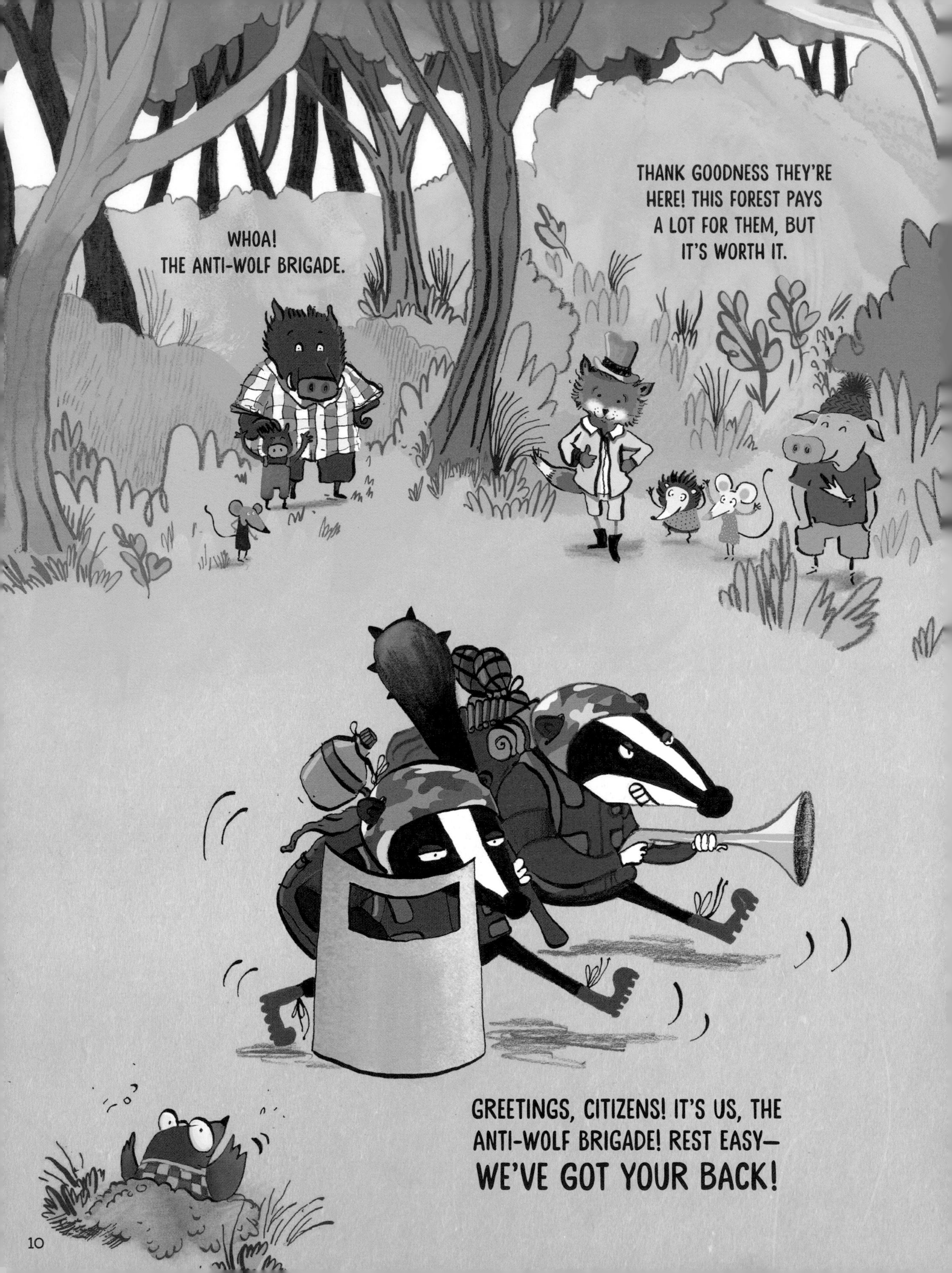
WHOA!
THE ANTI-WOLF BRIGADE.
THANK GOODNESS THEY'RE HERE! THIS FOREST PAYS A LOT FOR THEM, BUT IT'S WORTH IT.
GREETINGS, CITIZENS! IT'S US, THE ANTI-WOLF BRIGADE! REST EASY— WE'VE GOT YOUR BACK!

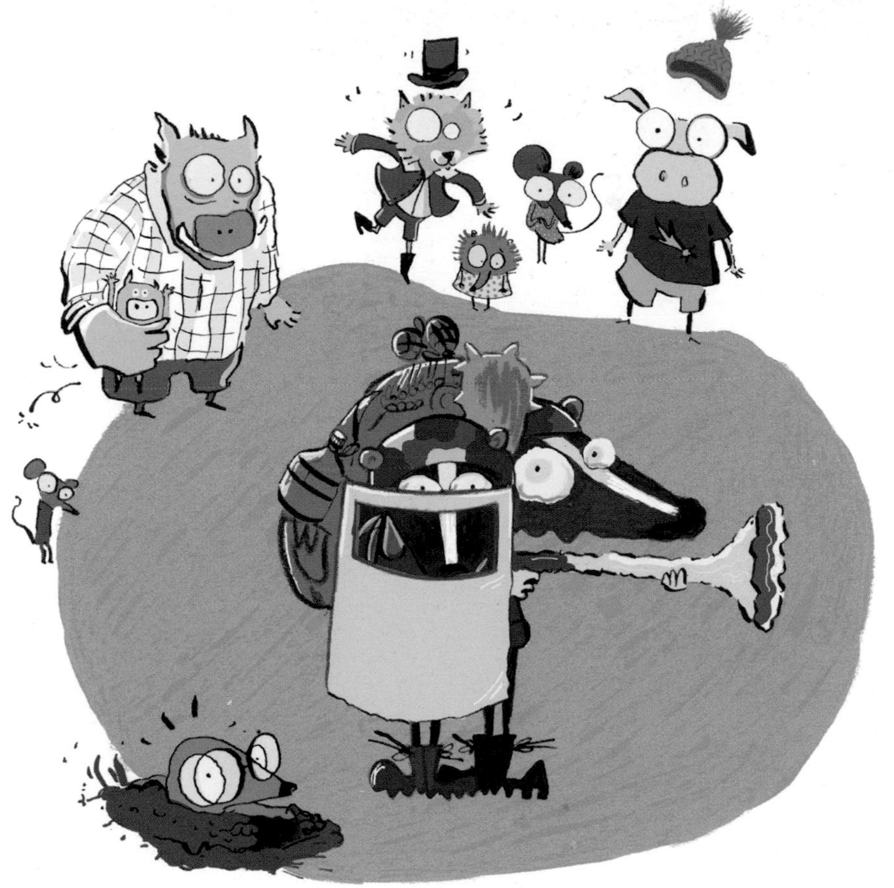

HERE COMES THE **WOLF!!!**

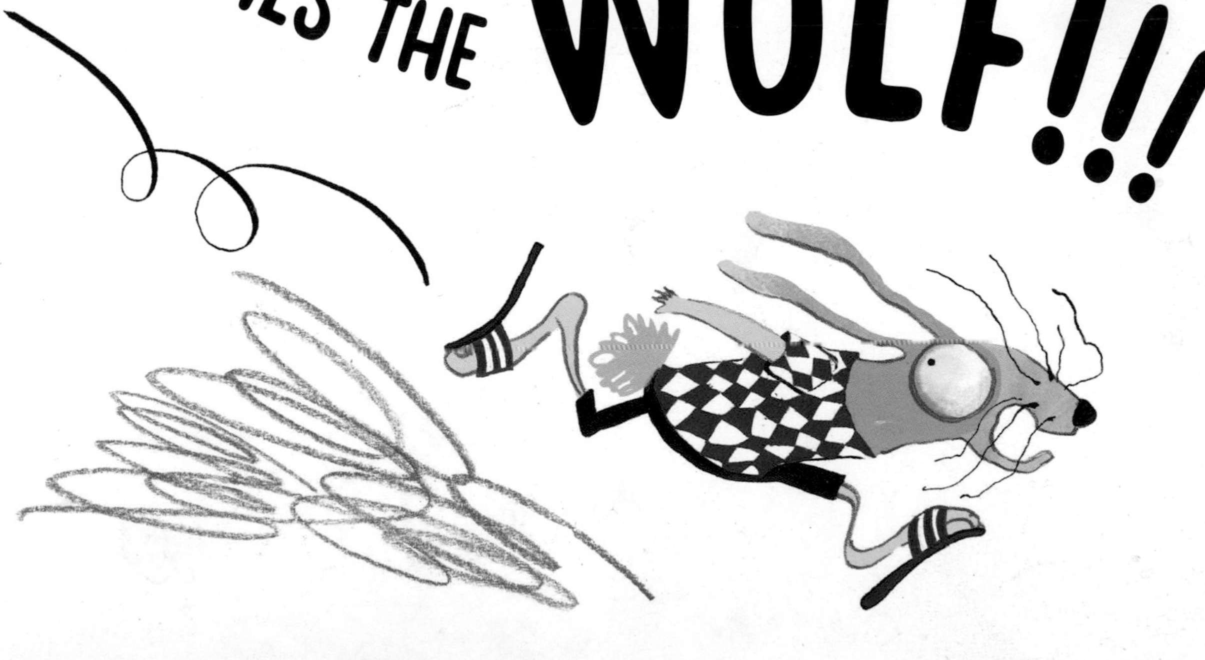

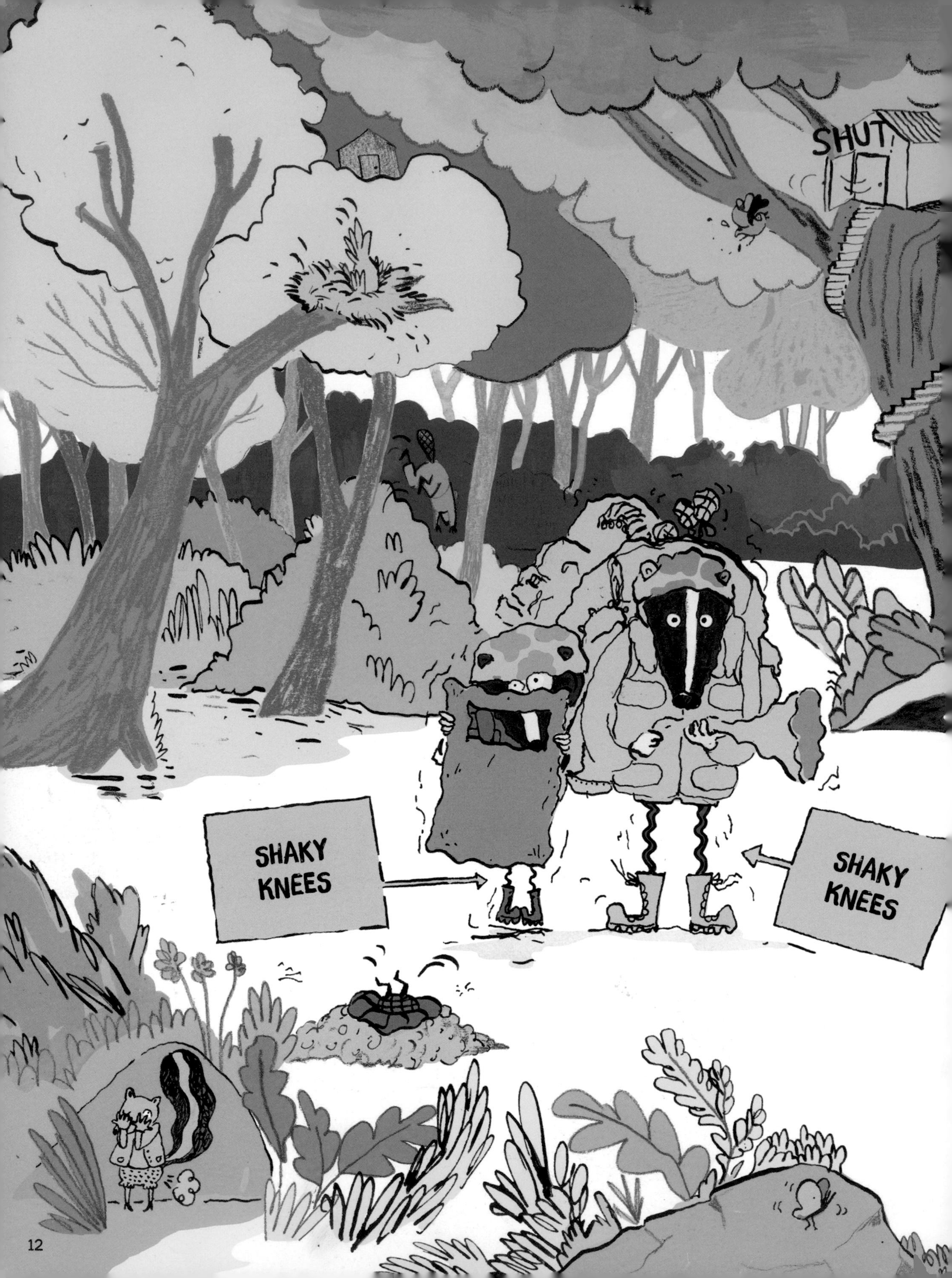
SHUT
SHAKY KNEES
SHAKY KNEES

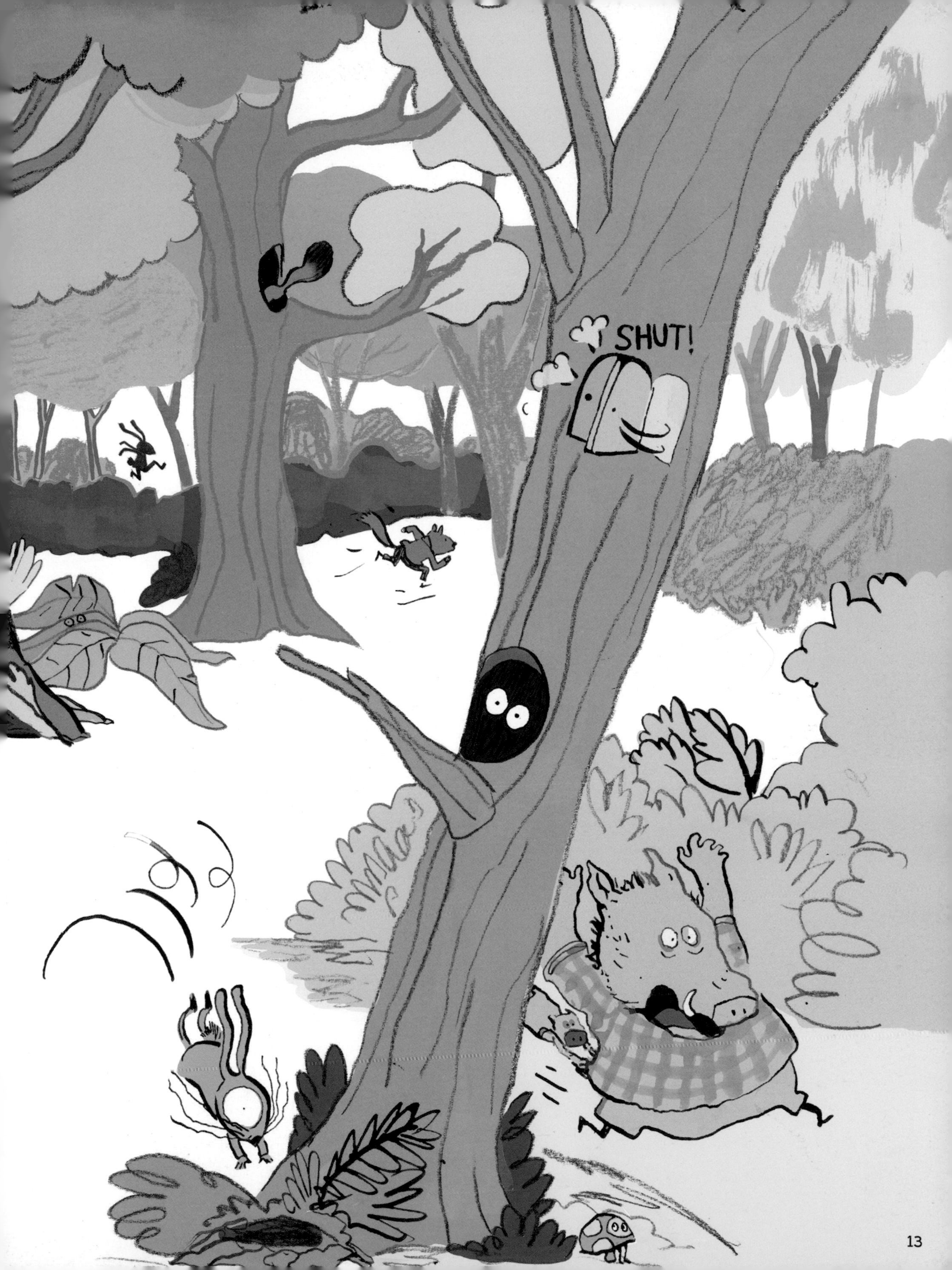
SHUT!

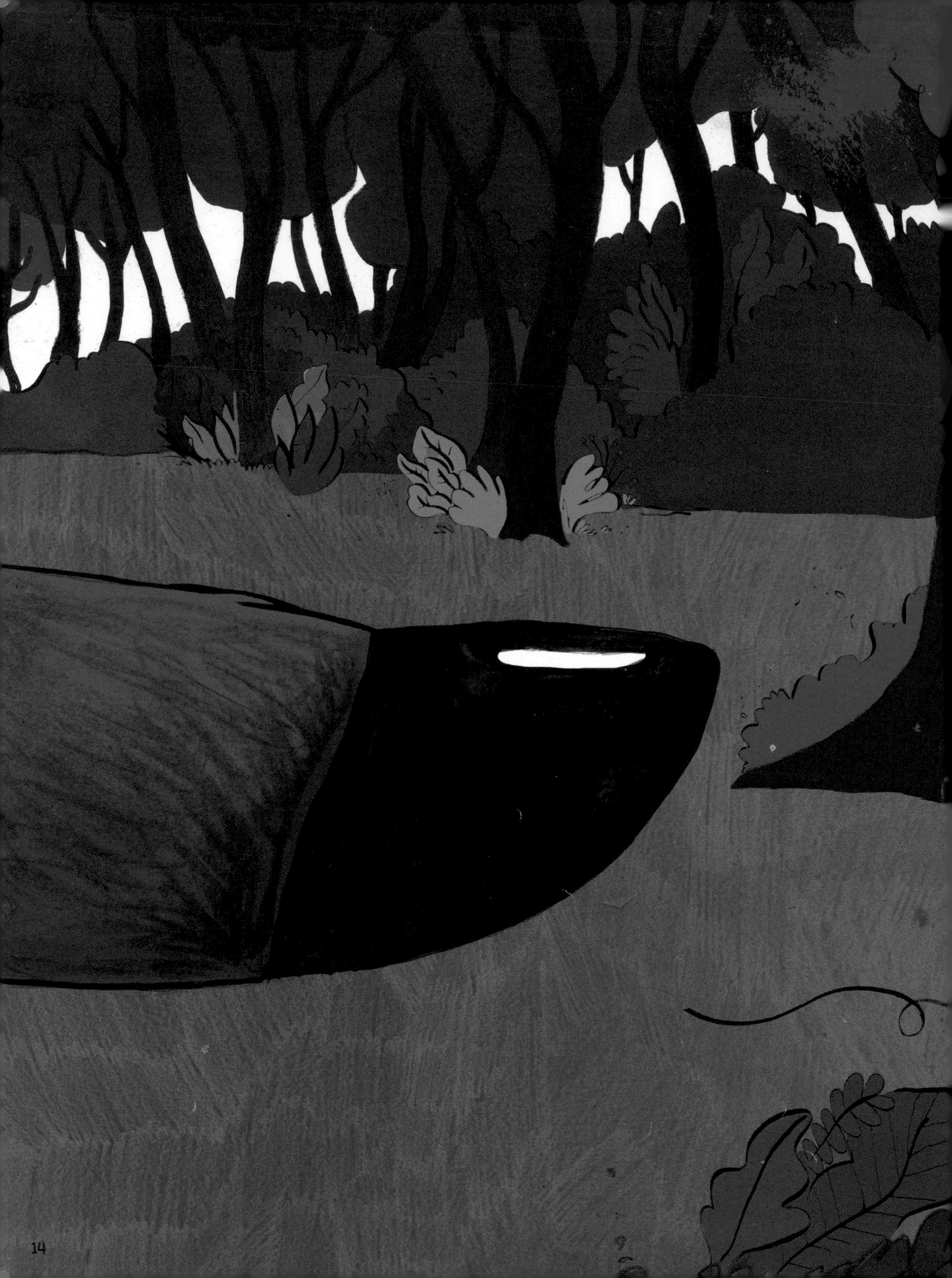

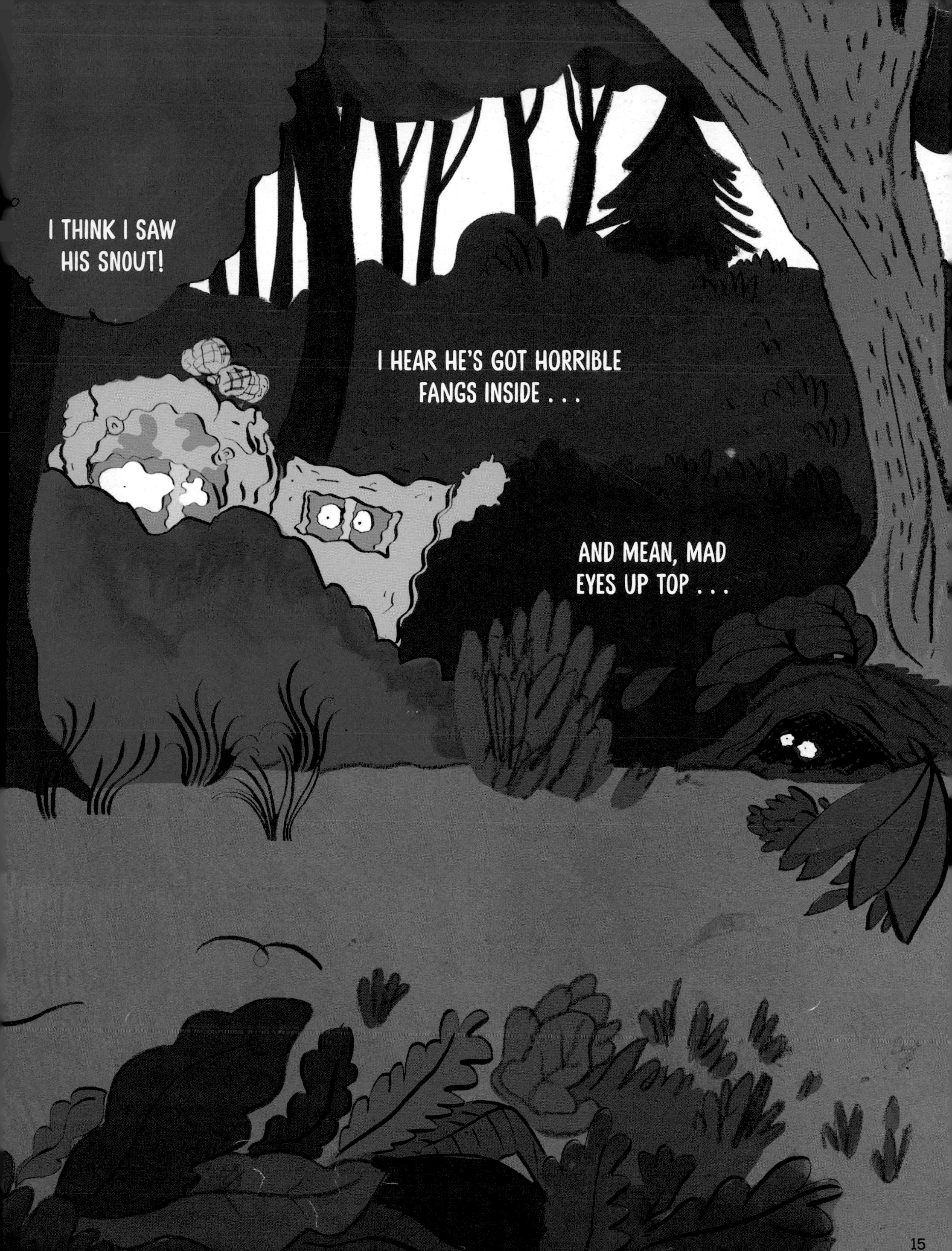

I THINK I SAW HIS SNOUT!
I HEAR HE'S GOT HORRIBLE FANGS INSIDE . . .
AND MEAN, MAD EYES UP TOP . . .

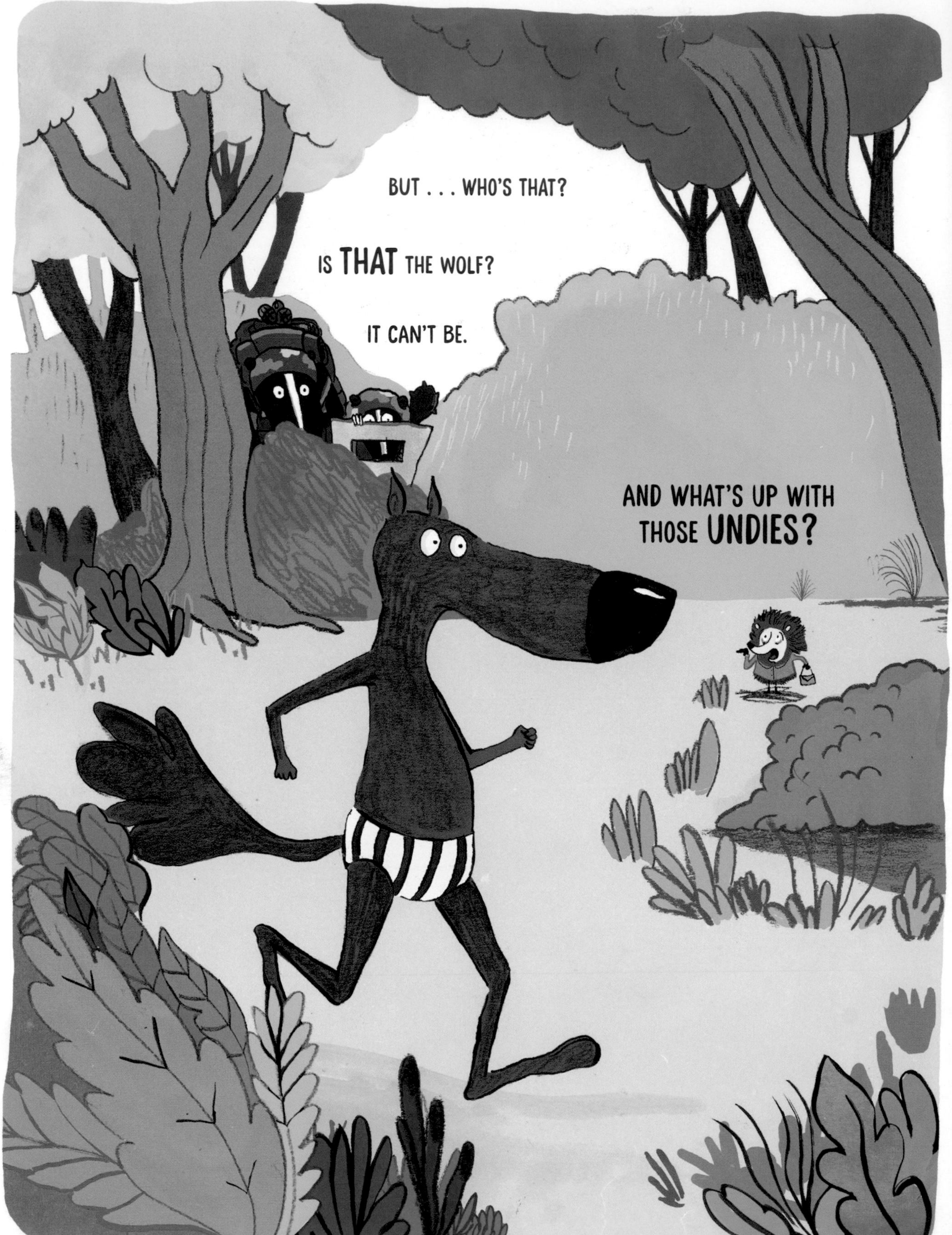
BUT . . . WHO'S THAT?
IS THAT THE WOLF?
IT CAN'T BE.
AND WHAT'S UP WITH THOSE UNDIES?

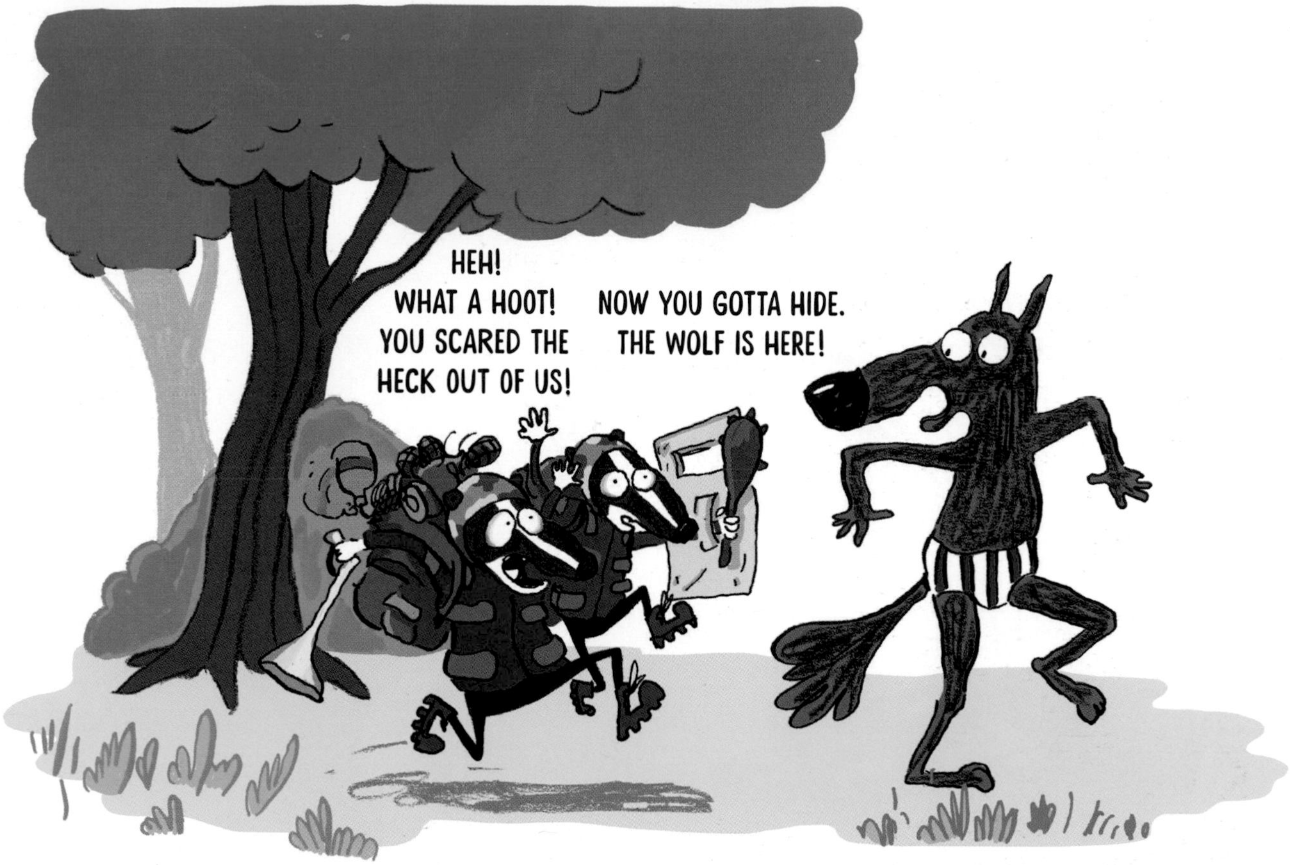
HEH!
WHAT A HOOT!
YOU SCARED THE
HECK OUT OF US!
NOW YOU GOTTA HIDE.
THE WOLF IS HERE!

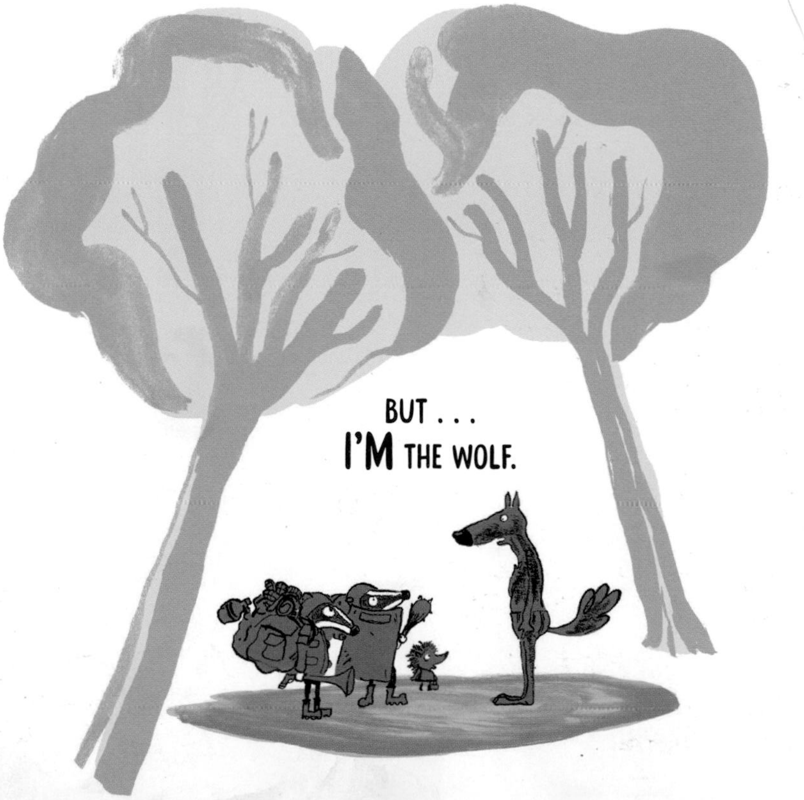
BUT . . .
I'M THE WOLF.

19

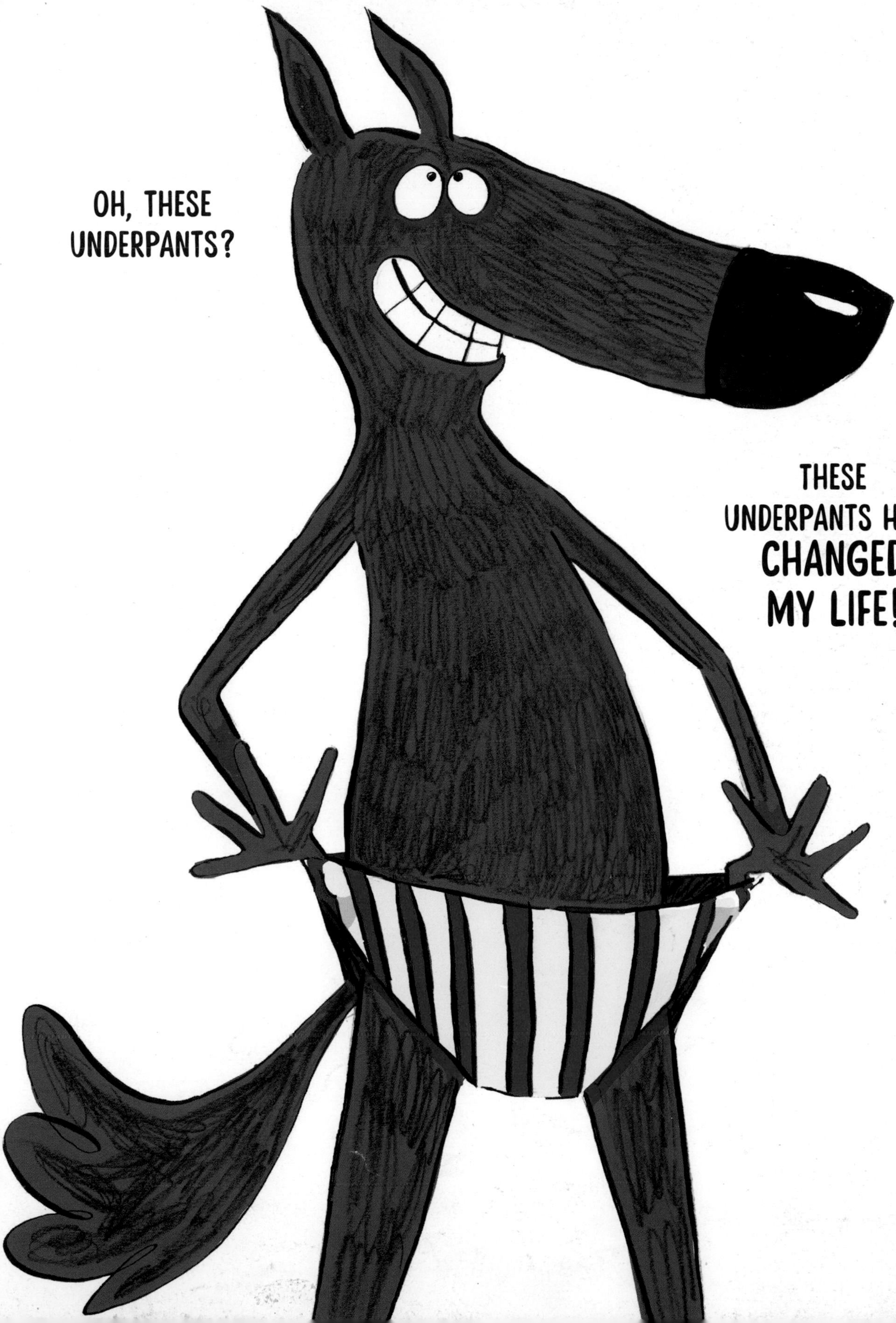
OH, THESE UNDERPANTS?
THESE UNDERPANTS HAVE CHANGED MY LIFE!

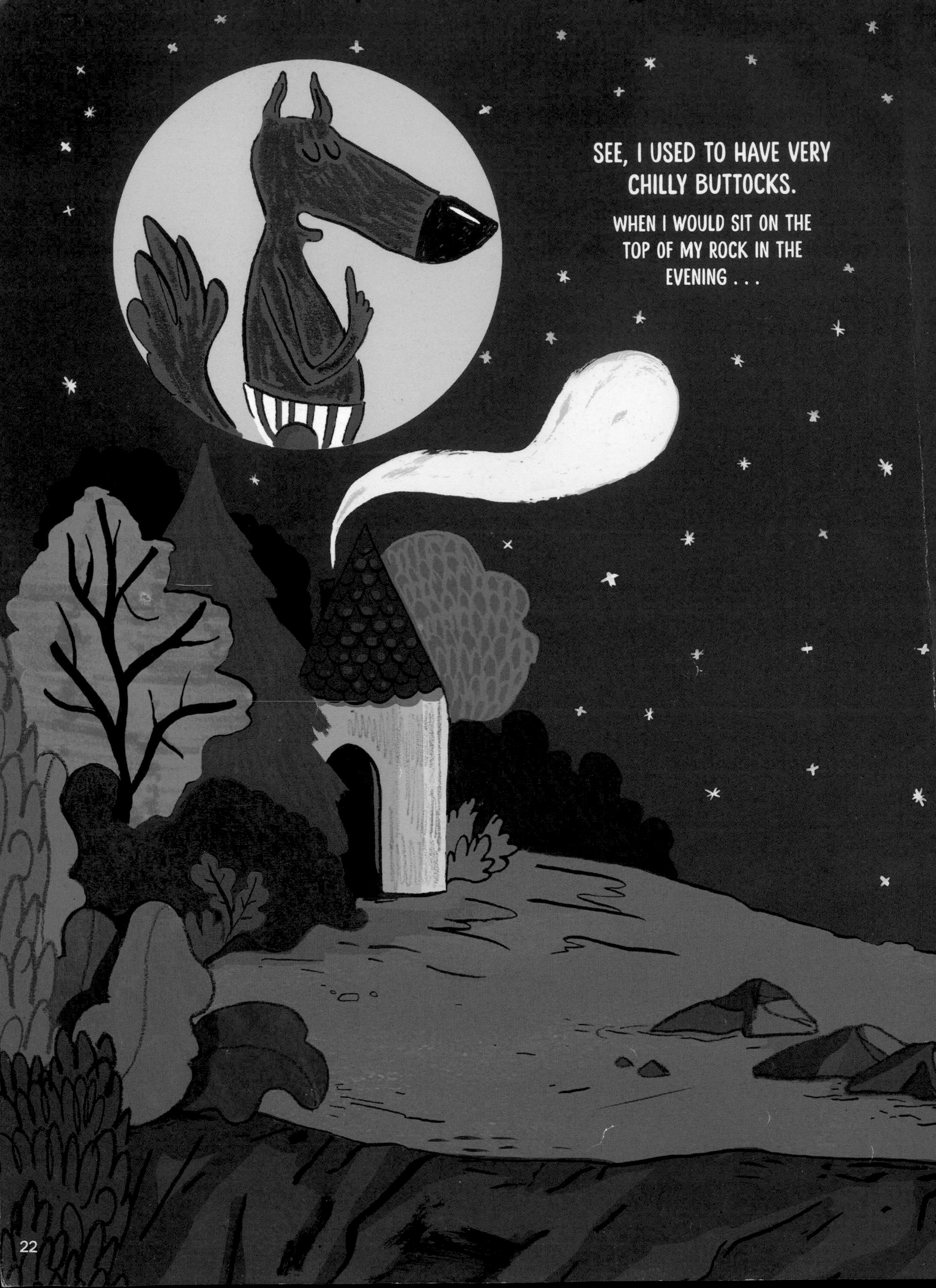
SEE, I USED TO HAVE VERY CHILLY BUTTOCKS.
WHEN I WOULD SIT ON THE TOP OF MY ROCK IN THE EVENING . . .

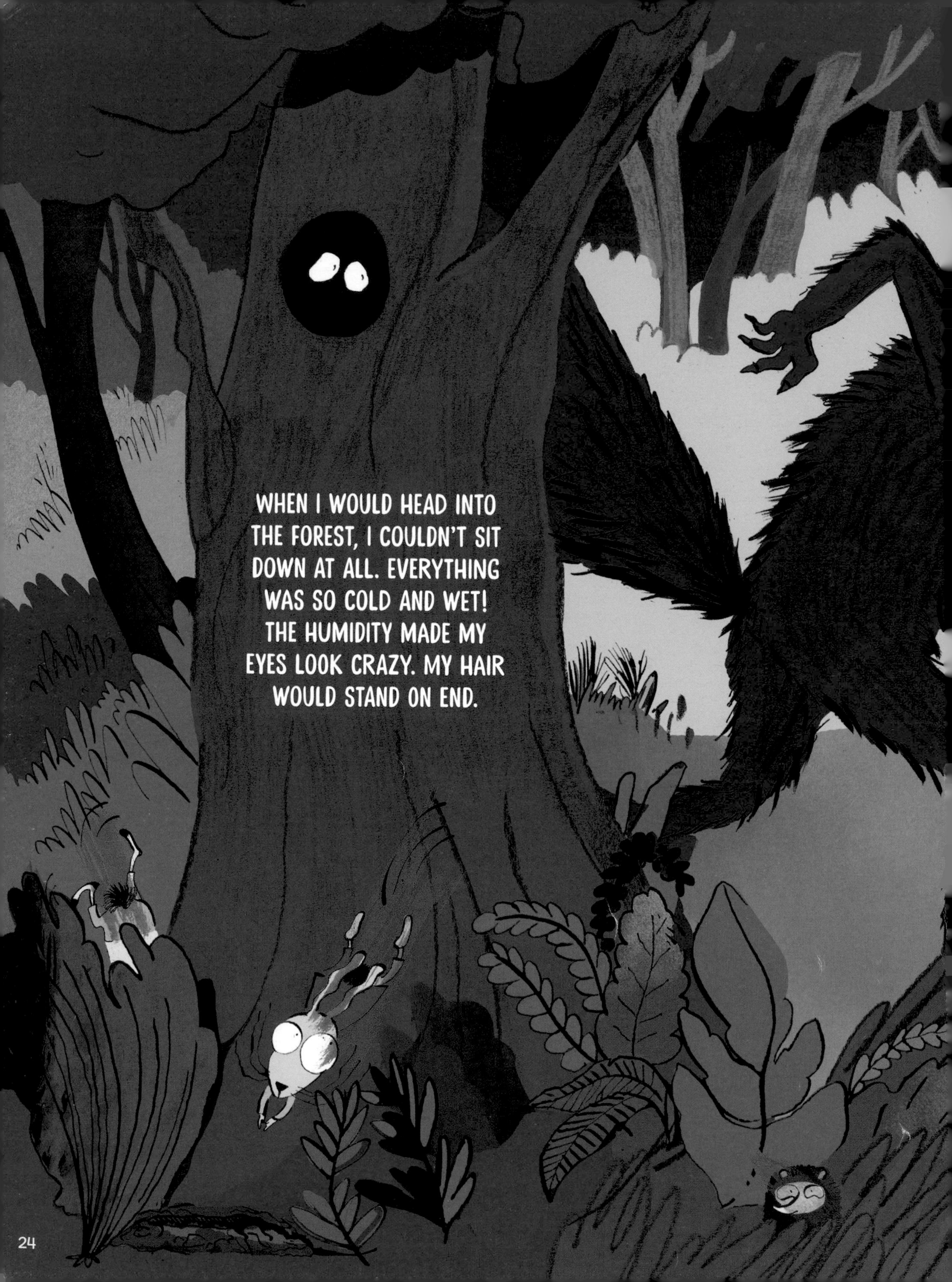

WHEN I WOULD HEAD INTO THE FOREST, I COULDN'T SIT DOWN AT ALL. EVERYTHING WAS SO COLD AND WET! THE HUMIDITY MADE MY EYES LOOK CRAZY. MY HAIR WOULD STAND ON END.

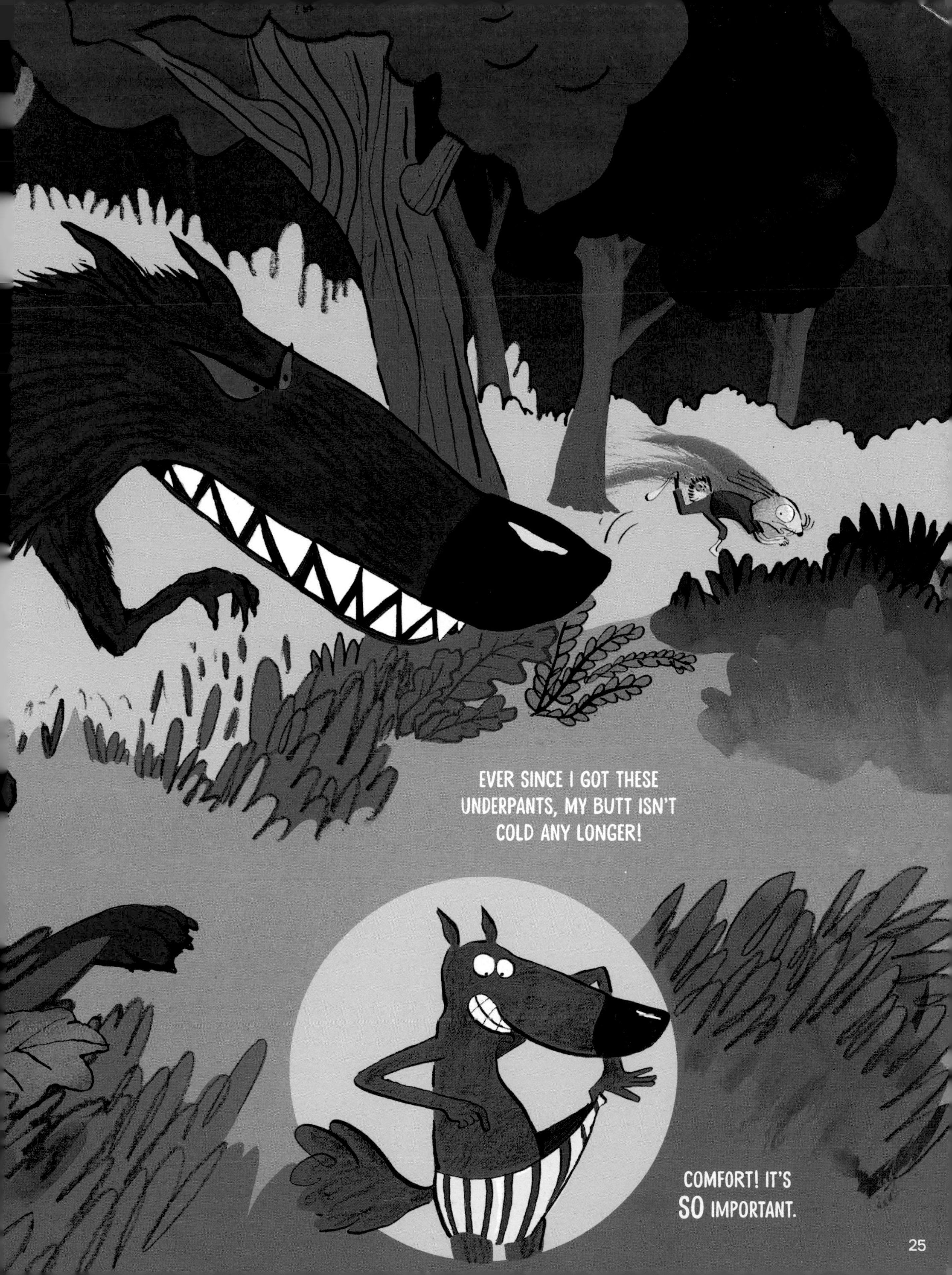
EVER SINCE I GOT THESE UNDERPANTS, MY BUTT ISN'T COLD ANY LONGER!
COMFORT! IT'S SO IMPORTANT.

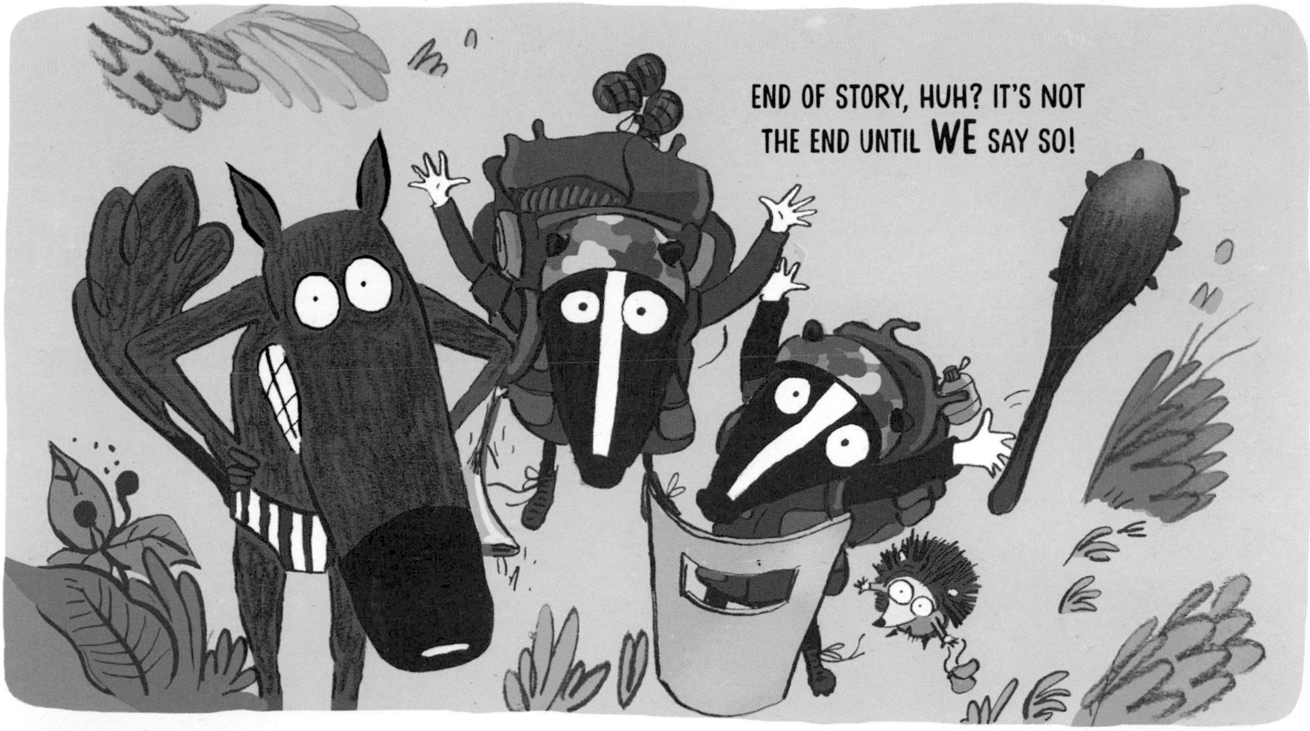
END OF STORY, HUH? IT'S NOT THE END UNTIL WE SAY SO!

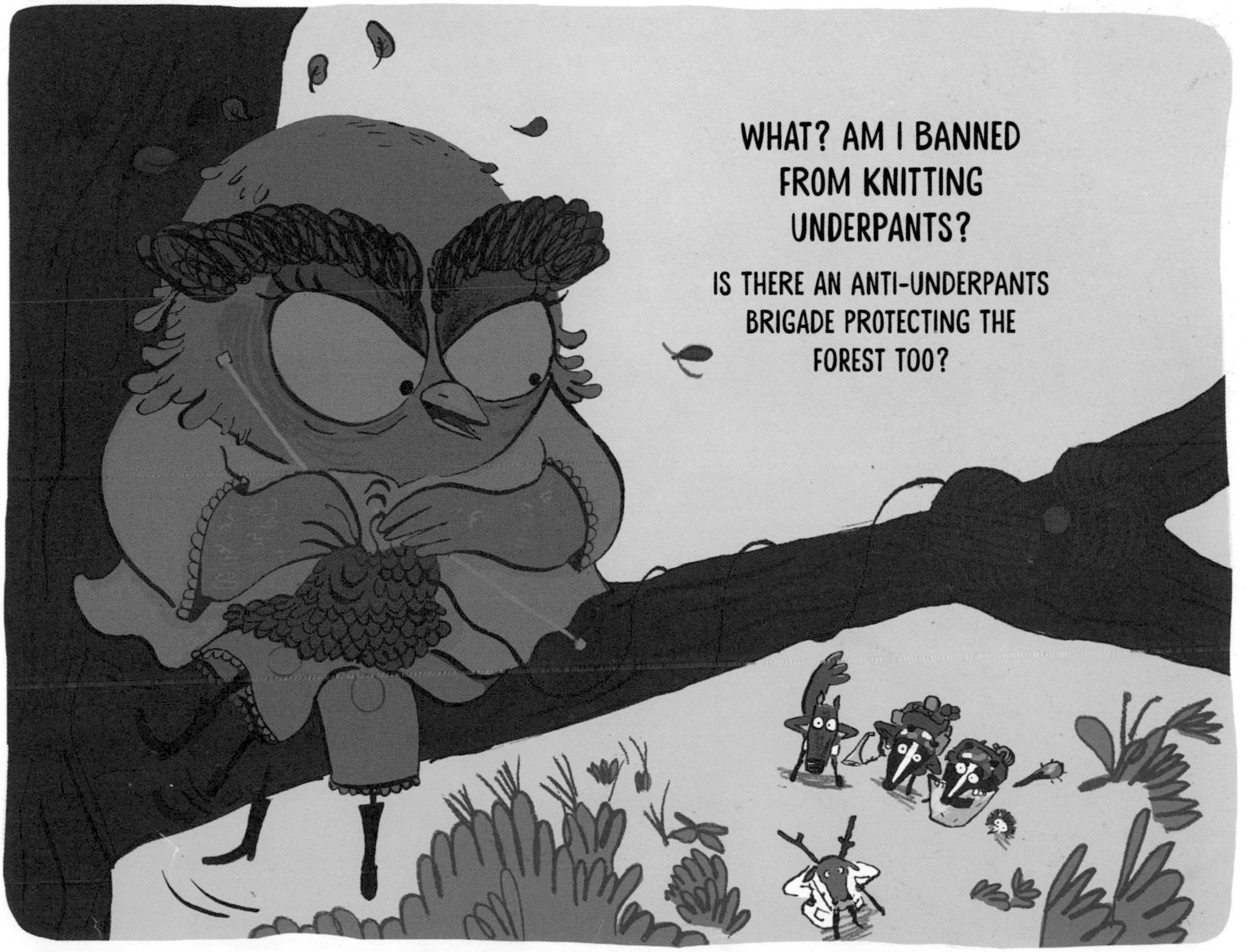
WHAT? AM I BANNED FROM KNITTING UNDERPANTS?
IS THERE AN ANTI-UNDERPANTS BRIGADE PROTECTING THE FOREST TOO?

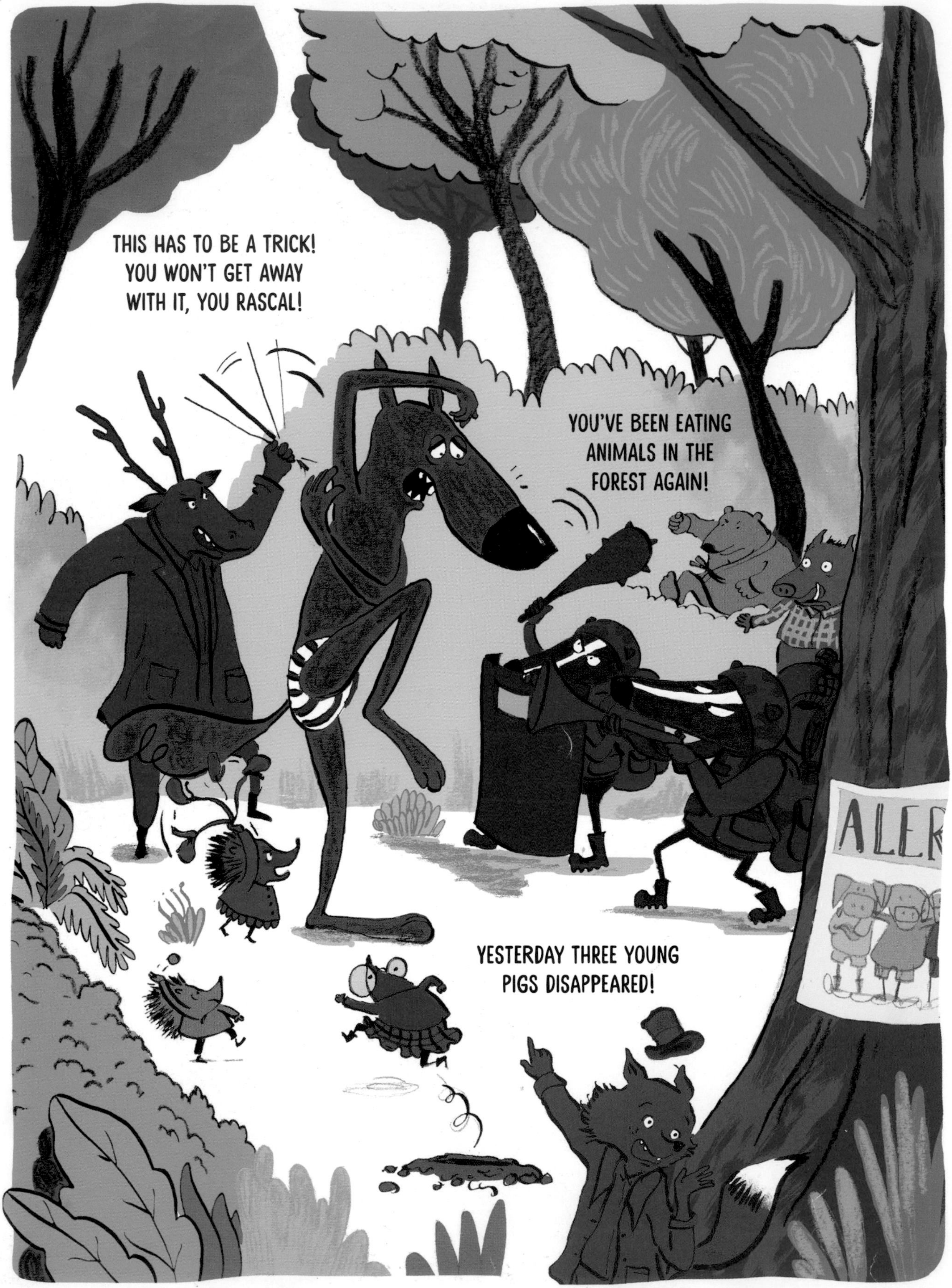
THIS HAS TO BE A TRICK! YOU WON'T GET AWAY WITH IT, YOU RASCAL!
YOU'VE BEEN EATING ANIMALS IN THE FOREST AGAIN!
YESTERDAY THREE YOUNG PIGS DISAPPEARED!
ALER

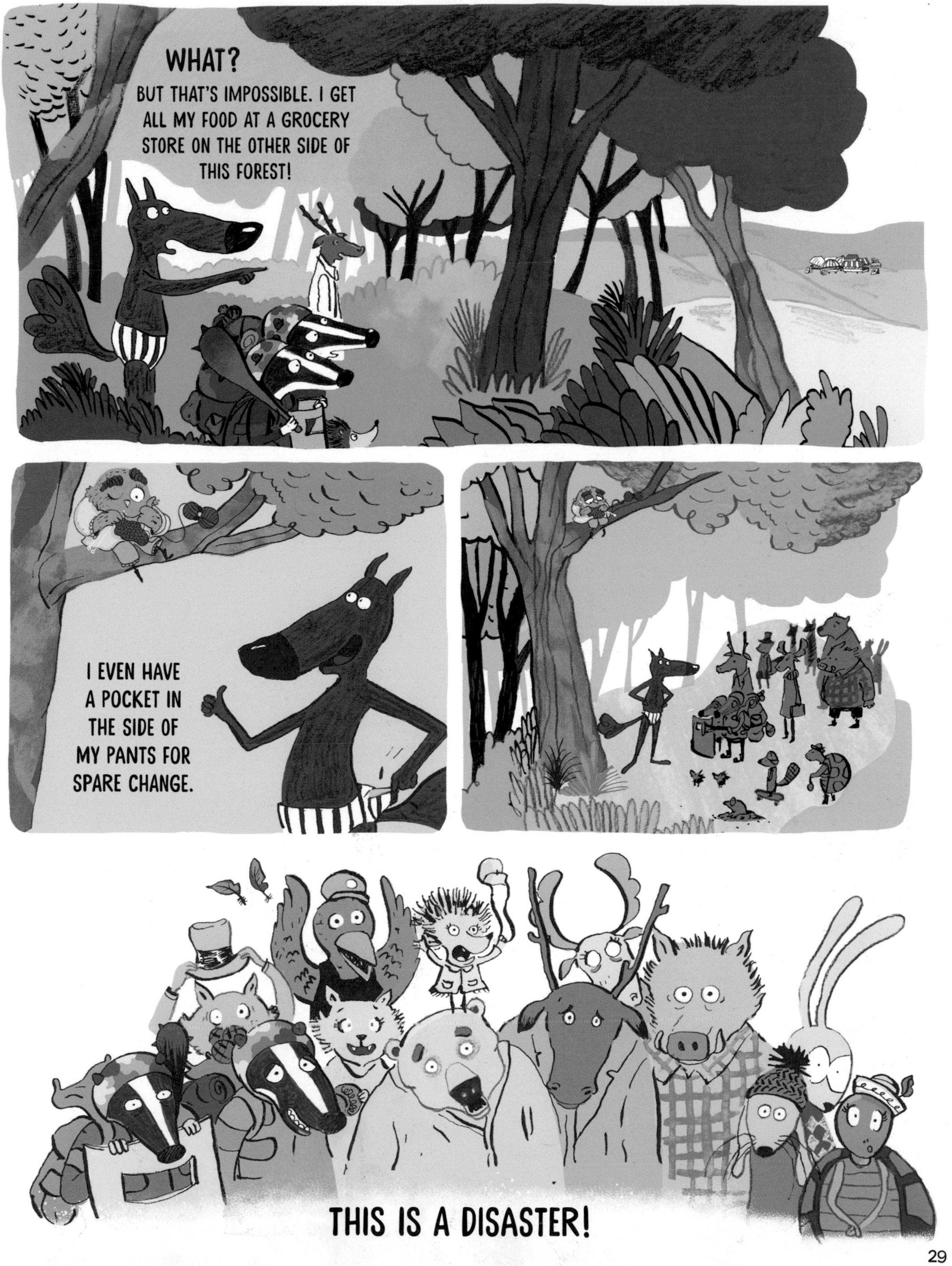

WHAT?
BUT THAT'S IMPOSSIBLE. I GET ALL MY FOOD AT A GROCERY STORE ON THE OTHER SIDE OF THIS FOREST!
I EVEN HAVE A POCKET IN THE SIDE OF MY PANTS FOR SPARE CHANGE.
THIS IS A DISASTER!

NOW WHO'S GONNA BUY
AN ANTI-WOLF FENCE?

AND WHAT ABOUT ME AND
MY SCARY WOLF LECTURES?

PLUS, WHO WILL BUY MY WOLF TRAPS?

THE *FOREST GAZETTE* HAS NOTHING
TO WRITE ABOUT WITHOUT YOU!

WHAT ARE WE EVEN
GOING TO **TALK** ABOUT?

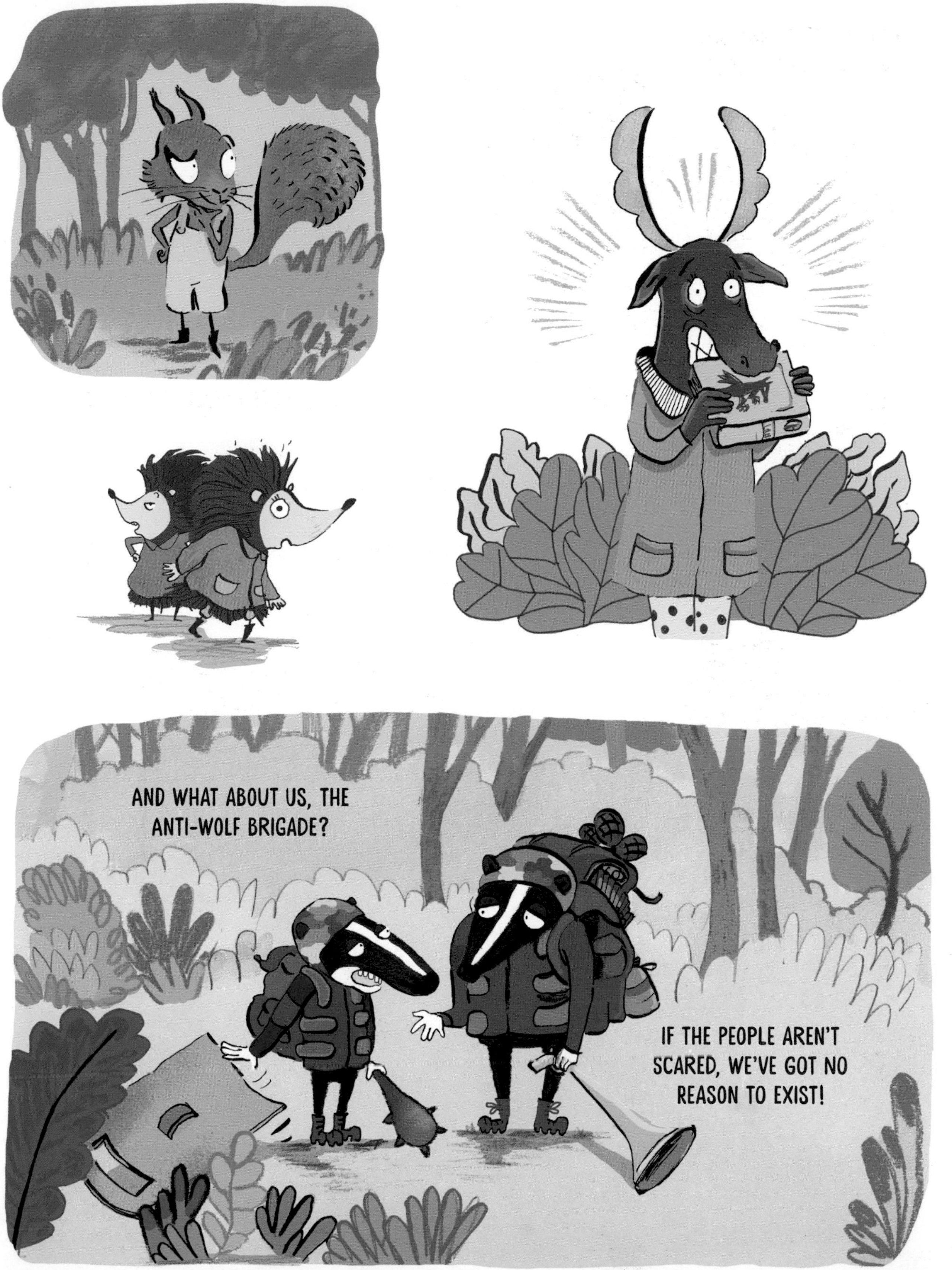
AND WHAT ABOUT US, THE ANTI-WOLF BRIGADE?
IF THE PEOPLE AREN'T SCARED, WE'VE GOT NO REASON TO EXIST!

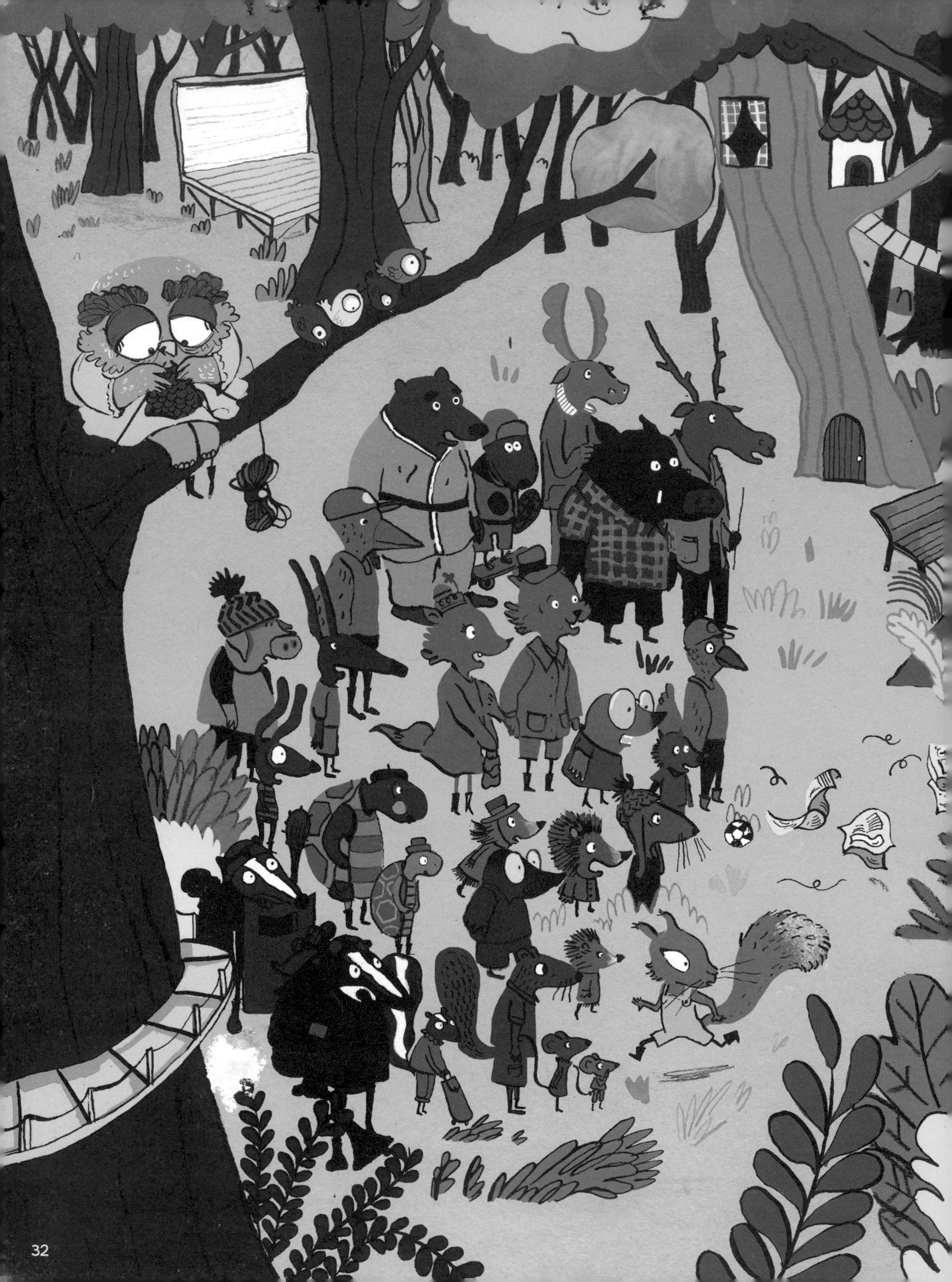

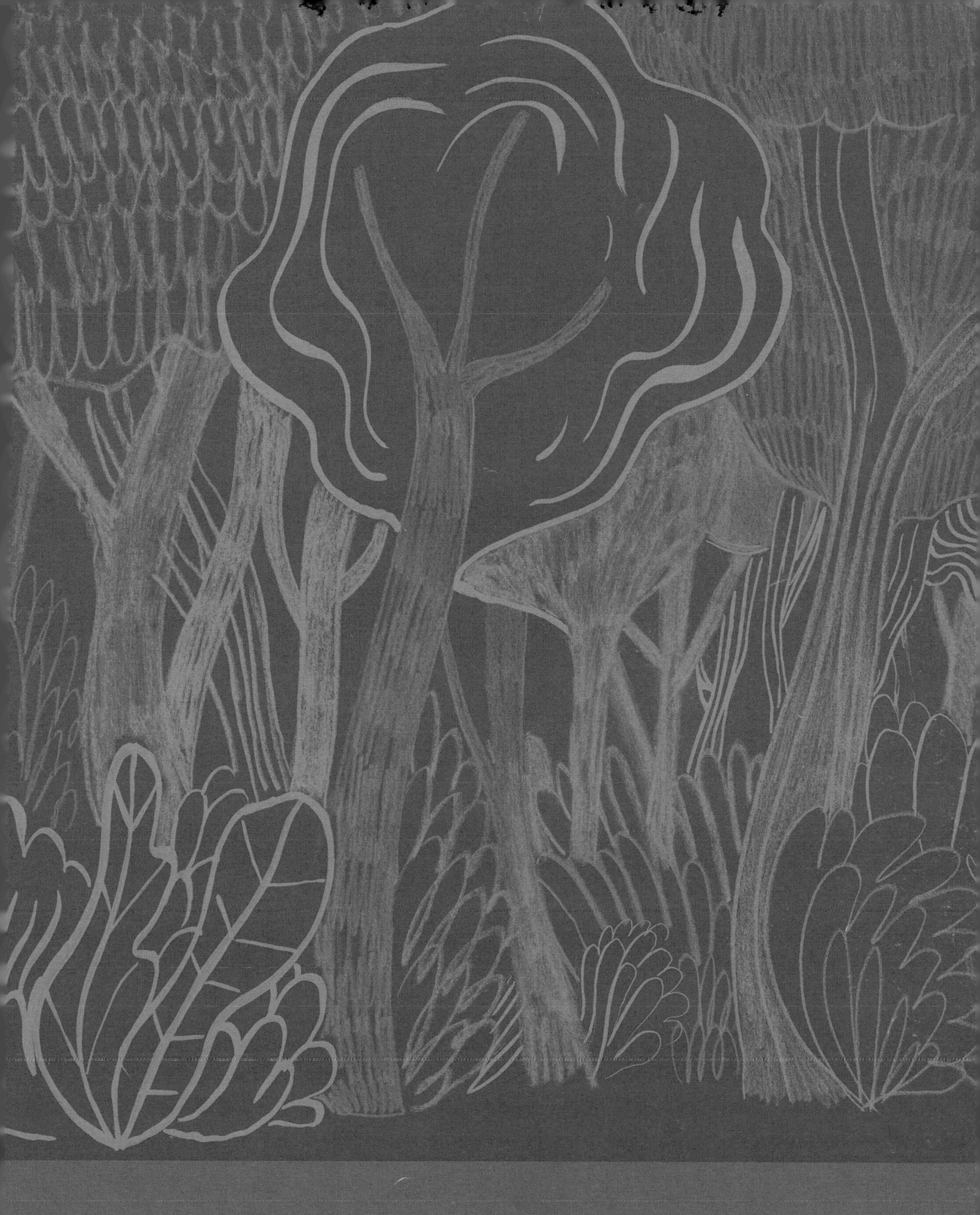

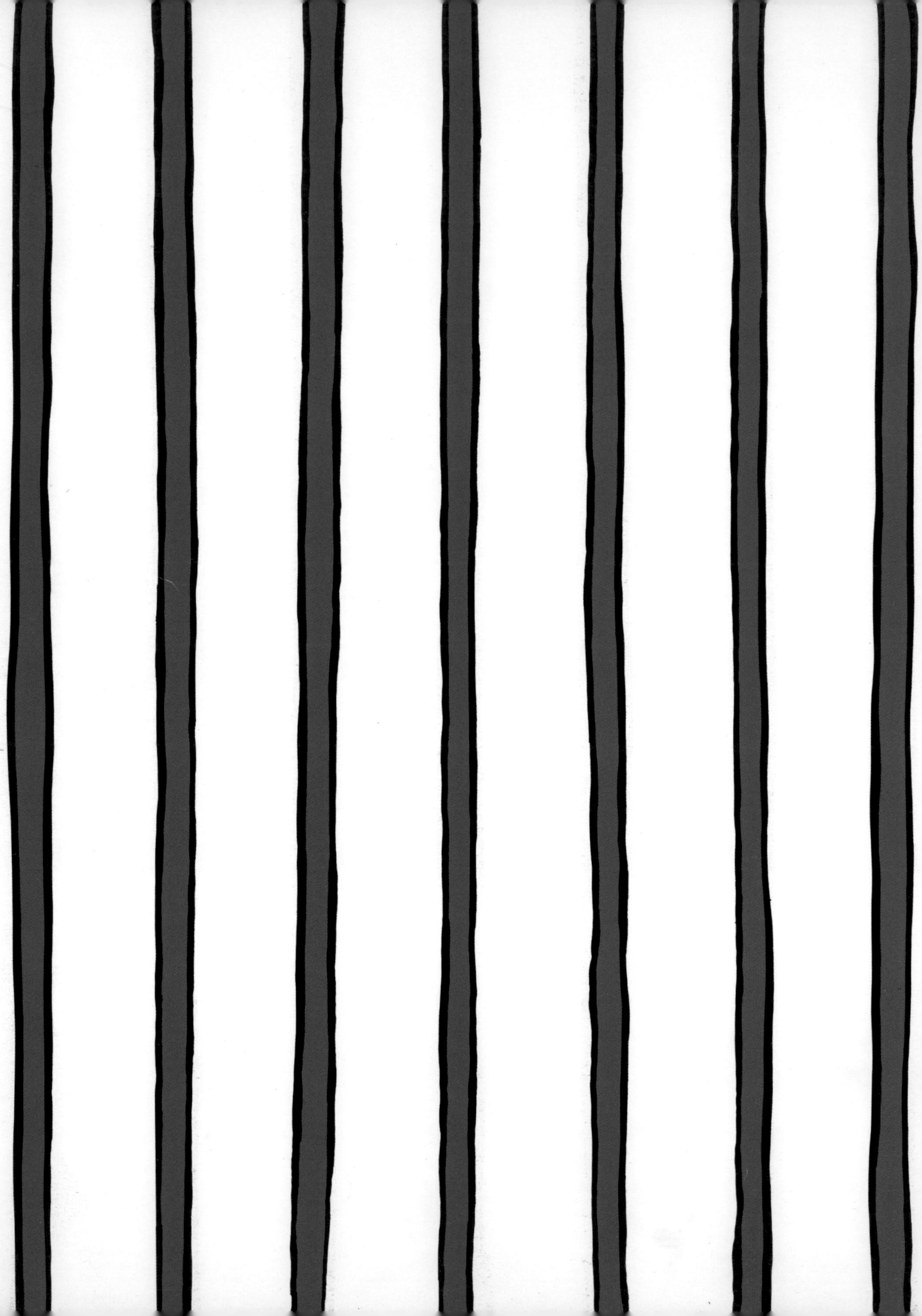

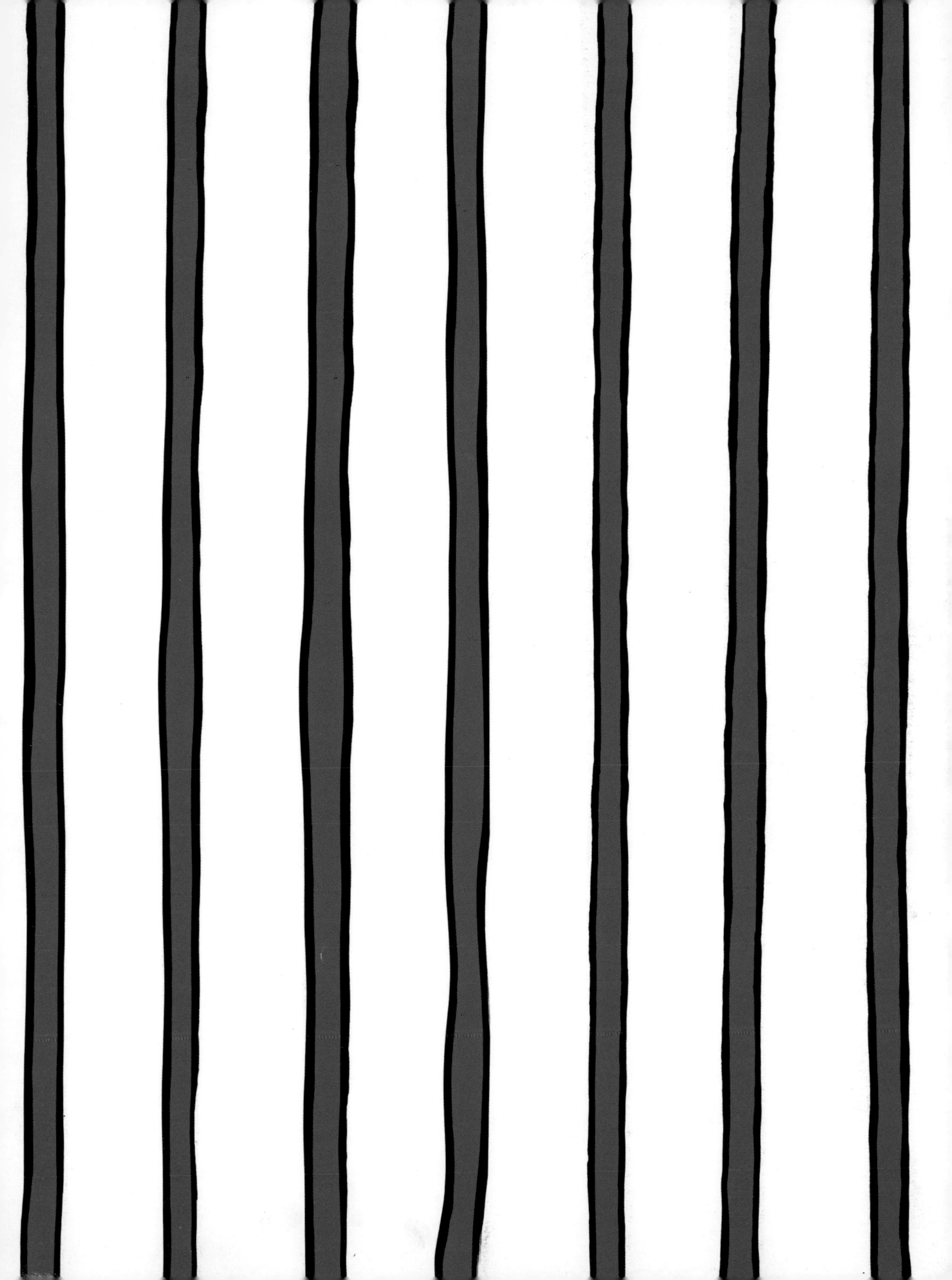